Hotel A

Hotel Aphrodisia

Dorothy Starr

LIBRIS

An *X Libris* Book

First published by X Libris in 1995

Copyright © Dorothy Starr 1995

The moral right of the author has been asserted

A CIP catalogue for this book
is available from the British Library

ISBN 0 7515 1287 7

Photoset in North Wales by
Derek Doyle & Associates, Mold, Clwyd
Printed and bound in Great Britain by
Clays Ltd, St Ives plc

X Libris
A Division of
Little, Brown and Company (UK)
Brettenham House
Lancaster Place
London WC2E 7EN

Hotel Aphrodisia

Dedicated to men who wear glasses . . .

Contents

1 Something in the Water

'*I DARE YOU*,' he'd said, and she'd told him not to be silly.

'I dare you,' he'd said, and she'd told him to go away, because she wasn't thirsty.

'I dare you,' he'd said, she'd told him not to keep going on, because it was all bullshit anyway.

The problem was Daniella Stratton hadn't been as sure of herself as she'd sounded, and those naughty, bespectacled brown eyes had been – and still were – irresistible. Not sure what she was letting herself in for, she'd taken the glass of water he'd handed her, and drunk down its contents – then rallied with more of her bravado.

'And anyway, Mister clever Mitchell, the famous 'magic potion' doesn't work on me. So don't hold your breath for a reaction!'

Four hours later, alone in the staff bathroom of the Bouvier Manor Hotel, Dani Stratton was furious. Still angry with Mitch for goading her; but even crosser with herself, for letting her nemesis get the better of her. Again.

Why the hell can't I ever say 'no' to a dare? she wondered with a sigh. And why on earth couldn't she cope with a smooth-talking, brown-eyed charmer whose smile was equally hard to say 'no' to? Stroppy, ignorant, or even flirtatious guests were a piece of cake to her – she seemed to have an inborn knack for diplomacy – but that bastard Joseph Mitchell? He seemed to get to her again and again.

Stepping naked and dripping from the tiny shower, Dani felt hotter and more bothered than she had when she'd first stepped in the damn thing. She never should have drunk that glass of water, not only because it was letting Mitch score a point, but because there was always the slimmest chance that the stories about the mineral spring were true. It seemed a silly notion, but Bouvier Manor Spring Water – the so-called 'magic potion' – was supposed to be an aphrodisiac. Dani didn't believe in anything that didn't have a rational, scientific explanation, but even so, she could feel something at work in her bloodstream. Her body was warm and tingling, and her breasts and her sex felt exquisitely sensitive – and all thanks to wretched Joseph Mitchell and his mind-bending brandy-brown eyes. Something was making her feel horny, and it was either the water or him!

Ah, but do you even have to drink the stuff? Dani pondered, looking up at the dripping shower head with suspicion. What if the effects were absorbed through the skin as well? What if there was some truth in the tales, and she'd been taking in the chemical – or whatever it was – every time she showered? She was beginning to lose all faith in her self-control . . . Which was exactly what that devil Mitch wanted!

The man was a swine! A beast! A gorgeous, macho horror! She'd seen him watching and waiting and grinning that flawless white grin of his, and it infuriated her. His pure, unfiltered lechery made her want to smack him in the mouth, and he just laughed when she caught him ogling her legs or her full, rounded bosom. What made it much worse was the fact that her woefully un-feminist half found his scrutiny flattering, and that *she* couldn't stop looking at *him*!

Not that there wasn't plenty to look at. Joseph Mitchell had started at the Bouvier Manor two weeks ago – in the junior reception job that Dani had just moved up from – and immediately set female hearts beating. Dani thought it was something to do with him having a mature man's body combined with the face of a pretty young boy. He was the basic 'tall, dark and handsome' hunk, but his eyes were wicked and devilish, and he had a slow, cynical smile that kept him from being a cliché. Male bimbos didn't usually wear glasses either.

'I've got to hand it to you, Mitch,' she murmured thoughtfully, wrapping a thin, over-washed towel around her sensitised body and attempting to rub herself dry, 'If you weren't such an MCP, I'd make a pass at you!'

The most annoying thing about Mitch – and in some ways also the most appealing – was his total and unflappable calm. He was a teaser, and perfectly and infuriatingly insolent sometimes, but at heart she sensed he was dependable. He drove her crazy, but he was also a constant. A friend in times that weren't easy. The atmosphere at the Bouvier Manor was extremely peculiar these days because everybody was on tenter-hooks. The place had been sold, and there was talk of management shake-ups and a draconian

3

new regime. Nothing radical had actually happened yet, but it was only a matter of weeks before a faceless consortium took them over.

Mitch, however, didn't seem worried at all, and his outrageous good humour was a distraction. As was his raw, sexy cheek!

Sitting on the edge of the bath and pulling a comb through her long red hair, Dani could easily picture his smile. That filthy, roguish, woman-stripping smirk that made her poor body moisten and shiver. Especially when she merged that expression with the rest of him. With the muscles, the broad chest, and those lean, suggestive hips. He'd be an ideal catch if he wasn't so insulting, she thought, working her way patiently through a tangled wet curl. Even so, she still felt inclined to encourage him. His package alone was worth the hassle!

'Now who's being a chauvinist?' she muttered, leaping up again, her body wildly restless and hot. Her knotted towel slid subversively to the floor, and on the point of reaching down for it, she hesitated. The night was warm and her skin felt electric and glowing. She didn't want to be covered. She wanted to be bare and free and voluptuous, every part of her available and open. The image of Mitch appeared in her mind again, and she kicked the towel across the room in frustration.

They'd been playing subtext sex-games with each other since Day One, she realised. Flirting, eye contact, talking ever so slightly dirty all the time. It'd soon turned into an unspoken trial of endurance. He'd accidentally brush up against her; then she'd pay him back by subtly invading his space. And so on and so on and so on.

As a nervous sweat broke out in her armpits,

she imagined invading him now. Prising open the buttons of his shirt, wiggling her fingers inside, then stroking the warm plane of his chest. She'd seen him in the hotel gym only yesterday, and the body beneath the clothes was every bit as exciting as she'd hoped for. Solid shoulders and pectorals; flat stomach; thighs ... Oh boy, those thighs! They were like long living slabs of tanned power; and she could almost feel them pressed against her now, flexing in a slow, steady rhythm as he thrust into her again and again.

'Dani! Cool it for God's sake!' she cried, knowing it was already hopeless. She tried to eject Mitch from her thoughts, then almost as suddenly let him in again. With a sharp sigh of recognition, she saw him as she'd seen him yesterday, in the gym. Half-naked, snarling with effort, and perspiring. A pair of thin, marl shorts scarcely covered his modesty, and the rest of him was shining and bare. Except – and this puzzled her – that he still had on his glasses. Those elegant, metal-framed specs of his, that made his bright eyes seem brighter than ever.

The thought of Mitch's eye-wear made Dani smile in her reverie. She sat down again on the bath's edge, and peered into the mirror on the wall beside her. Rubbing away the veil of steam, she studied her image, smoothing her wet red hair out of her eyes ... Eyes that were always hidden behind contact lenses; not because they were in anyway defective – her vision was perfect – but because fate, or her genes, or whatever, had chosen to give her one blue eye and one that was brown.

Dani found her idiosyncratic eyes quite attractive – they gave character to a conventionally pretty face – but she knew that other

5

people found them strange. Mitch, she suspected, would make a big joke of them, and find a way to make the humour sexual. He did this, as a rule, with most things – and with *everything* that had to do with her!

Still in the grip of her fantasy, Dani slid off her cool, narrow perch and lay down on the nubbly old bathmat. What she was about to do was madness, pure madness, but she was wallowing helplessly in desire. A hunger that wouldn't let her think. . .

Closing her eyes, she studied the dark screen behind her eyelids, then saw herself and Mitch here together, face to face in this small steam-filled room. He was sitting on the flipped-down lid of the lavatory – his body nude and totally relaxed. His skin was damp with moisture, his long muscular thighs were parted, and his dark eyes were intent behind his glasses. He was gazing downwards; down towards the beautiful, gleaming erection that jutted up from his loins like a tower.

Dani had never seen Mitch's penis, but in the gym his skimpy shorts hadn't hidden much. It was a simple matter to extrapolate, to use her wishful, lustful thinking, and build a picture of his masculine glory.

In silent abstraction, her mirage began to stroke his own member, teasing it with slowly sliding fingers to an even greater hardness and redness. Watching, knowing he was a dream but not caring, Dani stirred her bottom uneasily on the bathmat while her inner self rose up, crossed the room and stood over Mitch. His thick, yearning rod seemed to twitch at her in greeting, and as if reading his own flesh, Mitch looked up, his eyes desperate and pleading in an expression she'd never seen before.

6

He was begging her to have mercy on him, she realised. Humbly offering her his body, making it ready as both a tribute to her loveliness and an implement to furnish her with pleasure. In both imagination and dream, Dani felt her vulva grow heavy and liquid. She wanted him, and that was no fantasy at all. As her fingers stole down towards her centre, Mitch's brown eyes lit up with new hope.

What Dani imagined now was so intense and vivid that she could almost believe she was living it. To all intents and purposes, she stood before him, touching her own body delicately and for her own pleasure, while *he* continued to suffer for its beauty. His penis looked so hard it must be painful; yet still he continued to rub it furiously, his hips bucking upwards and towards her, and his bare rump lifting clear of the seat.

Dani felt implacable. He'd been disgustingly sexist towards her, yet now it seemed he wanted her madly. More than anything in the world, she thought archly, yet he hadn't done anything to deserve her . . .

Why should she have pity on him, just because he had a perfect, almost godlike physique and a long and magnificent penis? She could make her own pleasure – she didn't need him. He was just a toy now, a living love-doll. A stimulating piece of male meat. Let him perform and entertain her and be done with it.

Back on the floor, on her bathmat, Dani squirmed and caressed her own body – shaking her head in confusion and denial, while dream-Mitch sobbed out his deep anguish.

'Please,' he seemed to beg – even though all Dani could hear was her own panting voice. 'Please,' murmured Mitch again, his slim pelvis waving and pumping and his erection dancing lewdly to its tune.

'No,' she whispered, and saw tears of stress glittering in his eyes. He was too far gone now – he needed the release she wouldn't give him – and that knowledge made her body sing with power.

Beneath her fingertips, her slick flesh fluttered, and she gasped. She was close too. She wanted what poor Mitch was begging for, and probably needed it even more than he did. Being as cruel to herself as she was to him, she pushed two fingers firmly into her body, and smashed her thumb down squarely on her clitoris. In her mind, she saw Mitch's handsome face twist in agony, and his tortured cock leap and start to throb. Silky, jetting whiteness shot out from its tip; impossibly thick and copious as it flew through the misty bathroom air. Dani watched it arc, sublimely, then begin to fall; and as it did so her own moment took her. Her real, pounding, pulsing moment, an orgasm so intense and fiery that she screamed out aloud in her rapture – still clearly seeing Mitch's slippery fingers and the thick spurts of his seed.

She saw his lips move too, saw him trying to speak – then suddenly, she heard him shouting loudly.

'Dani! Are you all right in there?'

The words were punctuated by a sharp, insistent knocking at the door, and the voice itself was knowing.

For a minute, nothing made sense, then with a whimper of horror, Dani drifted back down into her body. Into her rippling and still trembling body . . .

The worst and most embarrassing thing had

8

happened. The thing she'd almost been expecting. Almost wanted. She'd pleasured herself right to orgasm, and as she often did, she'd howled out her relief as she climaxed.

Yes indeed, here in the tiled, echoing silence of the bathroom, she'd shrieked like a banshee in her ecstasy – while its cause, the star of her fantasy, was standing just feet away in the corridor.

'Dani? Are you sure you're all right?' Mitch persisted, his laugh unmistakably salacious.

'Yes I am! Don't fuss! It's nothing,' Dani called out resignedly, then smiled. 'I just thought I saw something in the water . . .'

2   The Devil Down Below

'*NOTHING IN THE* water this morning then?'

Mitch's eyes glinted mischievously behind his glasses as he looked up from the register, and Dani felt a strong urge to slap him. To wipe the smirk from his handsome face with the flat of her wide open hand. But it was a new day today, she decided, and she would stay in control from now on.

'No, nothing whatsoever,' she answered crisply, sliding around behind the desk and taking her place at his side. 'And there was nothing last night, either. It was just a trick of the light.' She moved an inch closer, daring him to back off – but knowing there was little chance he would.

'And anyway . . .' she continued, making it look as if she was checking the latest signatures whilst surreptitiously taking a deep sniff of Mitch's surprisingly expensive-smelling cologne, 'what were you doing lurking around outside the bathroom when you knew there was a woman inside? I know you're a pervert, Mitch, but do you really have to be so obvious?'

'I needed a shower,' he replied, all innocence.

Dani noticed him fiddling with a button on the bill printer, flicking it again and again in a most irritating fashion that she didn't think was good for the mechanism. 'I'd been running and I was all sweaty . . . I kept checking the bathroom door discreetly, but you didn't seem inclined to come out. Just how long had you been in there?'

The unspoken addendum was 'and what were you doing', but Mitch didn't ask it, because Dani suspected – with some horror – that in his own devious way he'd really known. Especially after the scream.

'Not long,' she answered airily, then frowned at Mitch's continued fidgeting with the printer.

'How long?'

'Long enough! Mind your own business! And what the devil are you doing with that?'

'Trying to fix it,' he replied amiably, crouching down to look at the control panel. 'Why so defensive today, Dani? Got something to hide?'

The change of tack, and the fact that his large, strong body was now pressed against the whole length of the side of her leg, shocked Dani into momentary silence. A silence that gave Mitch the advantage.

'You know, that didn't sound like a scream of fear to me at all . . . It sounded more like a scream of pleasure. I tend to hear a lot of those, you know,' he observed smugly.

You arrogant bastard! thought Dani, straightening the already straight register. She would have abused him to his face – or more correctly to the top of his head – but just at that moment Lois, the Assistant Manager, came gliding like a queen down the staircase, an expression of displeasure on her face.

Lois French was a beautiful woman, Dani had

to admit, but domineering. And this morning she looked decidedly both. Her sleek blonde coiffure had not a hair out of place, and made Dani feel dishevelled, in spite of the attention she always paid to her own immaculate turnout. The Assistant Manager's make-up was perfect too. A trifle heavy, Dani thought, especially with that severe blue suit; but even so, the red, red lips and darkly drawn eyes were compelling in a stern sort of way.

'Daniella,' the other woman said abruptly as she walked up to the heavy oak reception desk and stood before it, hands on hips, 'Has anyone been up to mend Ms Barrie's shower yet? She's been waiting since last night, and it really shouldn't be necessary for her to ring me personally about it!'

'I . . . um . . . I don't know,' answered Dani, feeling flummoxed as she always did by Lois's smooth, cold manner. She tried to kick Mitch, who was hidden from sight by the front panel of the desk, and whose task it had been to check on the shower. 'I think Joseph has it on his list of chores, but . . . but he's very busy, Miss French. I'm sure he hasn't overlooked it intentionally.' She kicked again, then swallowed and sensed the beginnings of a blush. Instead of coming out of his hiding place, Mitch was silently sliding further under the desk, tucking his body in neatly as he did so.

'Well, when you see him, remind him!' instructed Lois, turning round the register to check it.

At the very same instant, Dani felt something like the lightest touch of a feather running slowly up the inside of her thigh. It was a fingertip, tracing the sheer nylon of her stocking, moving

12

delicately over its welt, then settling on the bare skin above. She must've made some soft sound of protest, because Lois looked up again sharply.

'Are you all right?' she enquired, 'You look a little flushed. I hope you're not coming down with something. We all need to be right on our toes at the moment, you know. We're probably under surveillance already. The MJK Consortium is notorious for its sly management tactics. There's probably a mole here right now, watching every move we make, and taking notes. Checking us out for slack that can be trimmed.'

Dani listened to this harangue with only a tiny portion of her mind. She was too busy wondering what Mitch was watching, and what *he* might check out next. The exploratory finger was travelling rather measuredly over her thigh, as if testing the firmness of her flesh and the smoothness and softness of her skin. Dani was acutely aware of what lay at the apex of those thighs, and how handily it was placed for Mitch's studies.

'Are you listening to me?' demanded Lois, her blue eyes flashing.

'Yes!' Dani's answer was more of a squeak than a word, because in his hiding place, Mitch was efficiently easing her slim pencil skirt up the higher reaches of her thighs. She felt him bunch it at the level of her hips, an inch or two below the edge of the desk, then kiss the skin just above her left stocking.

'Good,' Lois said, not looking entirely con-vinced. 'Well, let's just go through the particulars of today's new guests. I want everyone pampered to within an inch of their lives. This is the worst possible time for complaints.'

Under normal circumstances, Dani would have

13

enjoyed a briefing like this. She loved working at the hotel, and found the eccentricities of their wealthy clientele endlessly fascinating. This morning, however, it was impossible to concentrate. She had all the fascination she could handle, and a dread of what might happen next.

She listened to words that seemed to be coming from a great, great distance, and answered them purely on auto-pilot; all the time conscious of her lewd and perilous situation. She was standing in a semi-public place with her skirt pushed up almost to her waist. Her only precarious shield was an ordinary wooden reception desk, beneath which a man was making free with her body.

She bit the inside of her lip as Mitch's fingers pressed lightly against the gusset of her panties. He was hardly touching her, but she realised to her profound shame that the fabric between her legs was already sodden, as if the fear was as exciting as the contact. Or perhaps more so. As Lois made some comment that demanded and received a response, Dani felt her tormentor press harder; using three merciless fingers to mould the thin cotton to the shape of her so it soaked up the moisture of her lust. In her mind she sobbed with pleasure, feeling him centre on her clitoris through her panties, then flick skilfully with the tip of his thumb. She was aware of her nipples hardening and swelling, and pushing against her bra and her white poplin blouse.

Would Lois notice that? she wondered hazily, almost wanting it to happen. Her jacket was unfastened at the moment, and with a slight movement of her shoulders she made it gape open a little. Down below, her clitoris got a long, lingering rub, and her thigh yet another soft kiss.

He's paying me back for last night, she thought,

as the folds of her sex began to quiver and she fought to keep her face bland and attentive. His fingers were scurrying about between her legs now, up to something; and dazedly, she shifted her weight, opening her thighs to give him more space. She knew she was losing it, and not thinking straight, because she suddenly realised there was no real 'last night' to be paid for.

'Now, I want you to be careful with these two,' said Lois, running a lacquered fingernail across two adjacent names in the register. Dani refocused her eyes as best she could, and looked down, feeling an *un*lacquered fingertip slide deftly into the leg of her knickers, displacing both elastic and lace.

'They're sharing the honeymoon suite. They're not married. And *he* looks about eighteen.' Lois's finely plucked brows described a significant arc. 'She's forty if she's a day, and loaded. But I don't want anybody implying there's anything unto-ward going on . . . Do you understand?'

Dani nodded, aware only of the progress of what felt like half of Mitch's hand inside her panties.

'Amy Lovingood's husband left her a huge fortune in properties,' Lois continued, her voice precise but very hushed now, as the first guests began appearing en route to the dining room. 'Consequently, it's not beyond the realms of possibility that *she* could be the power behind MJK. So look sharp, eh?'

'Yes, Miss French.' To her own ears, Dani's voice seemed to have no force at all. Her vulva was being fingered now, steadily and remorseles-sly, every small, swollen fold of it examined. She could almost hear the slicking of her own warm juices as Mitch stirred them and sampled their

15

texture. A cry rose in her throat, then died behind her lips as a second hand pulled down her panties at the back – almost baring her behind completely – then slid rudely into the cleft of her bottom.

Lois had turned away now, and was smiling a greeting to one of the guests, an extremely good-looking young blond man whose hair was long and tousled and whose face was vaguely familiar. Dani knew she should have recognised him instantly, but her mind was in a state of malfunction. She could concentrate on nothing but her crotch, and the way it was being violated, both fore and aft, by demonically inquisitive fingers.

He's that tennis player, she thought detachedly of the handsome blond. It's a shame he lost. I wanted him to win again . . . She tried to focus on the world-famous athlete, and remember his near miss at Wimbledon; but she couldn't. She smiled at him when he smiled charmingly at her, but in reality she barely saw him. All that was in her mind now was the trembling topography of her own troubled vulva, and the ministrations of a devil down below. The laughing-eyed Lucifer who was blowing on the hot, bare skin of her thighs as his forefinger pried at her anus.

This was the worst intrustion of all. More obscene and personal than anything he could do to her sex, a fact he seemed clearly aware of.

Above the desk, Jamie Rivera, the tennis star, smiled again. No doubt puzzled and intrigued by the languorous expression on the face of a hotel receptionist he'd scarcely exchanged a dozen words with. Dani's lips were parted, and she knew that her face must be pink and her eyes bright, but she was helpless, completely helpless. Mitch was gliding his fingertips repeatedly over her bottom now, always returning to her crumpled and forbidden little portal. It seemed to fascinate him, because each time he returned to it, he pressed into it a little further and harder.

It was almost impossible to keep her hips still, but Dani tried – fighting an intense desire to reach down below her waist herself. She wanted to either dash Mitch's hands away, or help him – by rubbing like a maenad at her clitoris while he worked more strongly on her rear. As it was, she picked up a pencil and pretended to toy with it absently – then almost snapped the hapless thing in two pieces as a finger pushed its way into her body.

At that moment, Jamie Rivera returned his attention to Lois – who was indeed quite worthy of it – and Dani was thankful for the very tiniest of mercies. She just didn't know how long she could stand there; trying to look normal, efficient and friendly, with a man's forefinger inserted in her bottom.

She didn't know which bothered her most: the indignity or the excitement. The way she was responding disturbed her profoundly, but it was something that seemed to happen often. If a lover caressed her bottom, she went crazy. Just the slightest little tease and her legs were thrashing, her hips bucking and her whole body wiggling and squirming and trying to bear down on the pressure. If she was touched there while a man was inside her, she'd orgasm almost immediately, gasp and grunt and cry, and be unable to contain her reactions. And if she was kissed there, or plagued by either tongue or vibrator, she'd scream and almost wet herself with pleasure, so frightening were the sensations she experienced.

Looking out on to the sunlit lobby, Dani could

feel Mitch's warm breath on her buttocks: wafting gently around the hole he was stretching and playing across the tissues of her sex. Her clitoris was a hard, aching button, almost shouting with a voice of its own that someone reach forward and give it attention. Watching Jamie and Lois move away, and sobbing an unspoken thanks to someone or anyone, Dani slid her hand slyly down into her panties.

Mitch's fingers tried to twine with hers and distract her, but Dani wouldn't let herself be swayed. Scrabbling wildly, she pushed her bottom back hard against Mitch's face, and took in more of his impudent digit. She felt him kiss one half-revealed cheek, lick it, then close his teeth in a playful mock-bite. But just as he pretended to nibble and gnaw the firm muscle, Dani's finger made the contact it sought.

She came immediately, and would have fallen but for Mitch effortlessly taking her weight. Her body throbbed furiously, filling her belly and loins with delectable waves of silvery, tingling warmth, yet at the same time she had a distinct, almost tranquil awareness of how uncomfortable her molester must feel. She was having an orgasm, the very pinnacle of pleasurable human sensation, while Mitch was crouched like a troll, part-way between her legs, his wrist and neck at two different, impossible angles so he could both kiss the smooth surface of her bottom and have his finger lodged snugly inside her.

Serves him bloody well right! she thought, suppressing a giggle of satisfaction when she was finally able to think – and even laugh – again. Deliberately, she let her body sag to increase his discomfort. She didn't feel sorry at all, and as several more guests passed by, she smiled and pretended to look down behind the desk, in search of some lost document or other.

'I hate you!' she mimed, as Mitch tumbled on to his side behind her, his finger popping out as he fell. Its abrupt leaving made her gasp, and under the guise of searching for the pencil she'd never dropped, she too squatted down behind the desk, making hasty adjustments to her clothing – and trying her best to elbow Mitch in the ear or the eye in the process.

When she bobbed her head up again, the lobby was empty. Thank God!

'I hate you,' she said again, her voice fierce as she looked down once more. 'You're a swine and a filthy, perverted bastard! I ought to get you sacked.'

Mitch just grinned, his eyes glinting behind his glasses as he lay back on the dull grey carpet, his fingers laced in a cradle behind his head. His thick, dark hair was slightly askew at the front, but otherwise he looked perfectly normal, perfectly sartorial, and unshaken in any way, shape or form. Dani thought about the sharp toe of her smart court shoe, but before she could use it effectively, her adversary had leapt lightly and gracefully to his feet.

'I don't know what you're complaining about,' he observed blandly, glancing over Dani's shoulder at the register, then without any warning whatsoever, sliding a hand right around her back under her jacket, curving it inwards around her ribcage, and cupping her left breast warmly through her blouse. She felt him heft its soft weight in his fingers, as if assessing its firmness and shape.

'Get off!' hissed Dani, and this time her elbow did hit home, stabbing Mitch efficiently in the midriff.

'Ouch!' he protested, dancing out of the way and rubbing at his wound.

'You should thank me, not try to maim me,' he continued, pretending to be aggrieved, but laughing at the same time. 'I gave you an orgasm in the middle of an otherwise very tedious conversation with the Ice Queen. You're very ungrateful. I was only trying to liven up your day.'

'If you don't get out of my sight this instant, I shall *end* your day, Mitchell, and end your miserable life with it. Now go and get Ms "best-selling authoress" Barrie's shower sorted out, will you? It might even be her that owns this place, if you think about it . . . They make millions, some of these writers, you know.'

'Yes, ma'am,' he answered smartly, sliding out from behind the counter, then snapping her a crisp but disrespectful salute. Still grinning, he walked away across the hall but stopped at the foot of the staircase and turned towards her again. 'And don't forget to let me know if there are any other little jobs you want doing. You know how good I am at fixing things . . . Getting into nooks and crannies and what have you . . . If you know what I mean?'

With that, he winked behind his spectacles, and Dani would have screamed the foulest of profanities – *and* told him he wasn't supposed to use the front stairs! – if a well-dressed couple hadn't just that moment appeared in the main entrance and started walking in the direction of the desk. Summoning all her business-school training, Dani smiled like the superbly efficient, conscientious receptionist she was, and welcomed them to the Bouvier Manor – while Mitch disappeared towards the first-floor landing.

20

The funny thing was though, when the couple were gone and on their way to their room, Dani couldn't even remember what they looked like. She tried, but all she kept seeing were a pair of twinkling brown eyes behind lightly tinted glasses. Eyes that went with a soft, deliciously evil laugh, and the sensation of sweet pleasure between her thighs . . .

And she didn't really hate him at all.

3 Literary Pretensions

AS HE MADE his way up the staircase, Mitch knew he appeared calmer than he felt. He certainly looked a damn sight more composed than his poor unfortunate penis was! Cramped inside his close-fitting underwear, it throbbed and trembled precariously as a result of his prank beneath the desk.

Shaking his head, Mitch pondered on his own stupidity. What on earth had got into him just now? He loved frequent and varied sex, and he adored beautiful women, but he didn't usually take juvenile risks. Especially when they left him unsatisfied . . .

It was Dani who'd sent him crazy, he decided. There was something about her, something unusual that touched every part of him. It wasn't just an erotic thing, his cock responding to her sex and to all the glorious femininity that went with it. Although her breasts, her bottom, and her legs were all spectacularly gorgeous . . .

No, it was her spirit that really warmed him. Her feisty resistance to any and everything that was likely to do her down: whether it was his own chauvinism – a trait he was sometimes truly ashamed of – or other factors, like that bitch, the hoity-toity Lois. The 'Ice Queen' was sly as a snake, and – as he'd discreetly observed – nowhere near as competent at her job as Dani would have been. Richard, the manager, was even less efficient than his second-in-command and shouldn't have been let loose to run a hen-hut, much less a five-star hotel in the country with a nationwide reputation for excellence.

And the Bouvier Manor must certainly be one of the finest establishments of its type in England, Mitch observed, reaching the first-floor landing and admiring the subdued but luxurious decor. The pictures on the walls to either side of him were all excellent works by minor masters, and he tried to distract his attention from his erection by doing some quick estimates of their value.

Although he had intended to go straight to Pandora Barrie's room, he hesitated before a canvas by one of the lesser known Pre-Raphaelites, then realised he'd made a huge mistake. The woman in the painting was curvaceous, dramatic, and redheaded – a typical subject for the Brotherhood – and reminded him poignantly of Dani.

His hand stole to his crotch as he pictured his captivating colleague in a sumptuous flowing gown, instead of her crisp, grey suit. His fingers closed firmly on his cock – through his trousers – as he imagined her *out* of the gown again, and naked and writhing beneath him. He could almost feel her satin flesh gripping him, and the shape of her sensitive, apple-shaped buttocks as he clasped them in his hands and sharpened the angle of his thrusts. She'd like that, he knew she would; it was his shameless toying with her bottom that had triggered her climax this morning.

Shifting from one foot to the other, and unselfconsciously stroking himself, he considered a detour to his room. For comfort's sake . . . There were one or two other things he had to sort out too, but five minutes spent caressing his penis would surely make his mind work more clearly. He thought of the delicious moment of completion, then knew that right now it would be little more than ashes. He didn't *want* to come alone, he wanted to share it with Dani. Or if not her, at least some other woman. Unbidden, he remembered his errand, and seemed to see again the rather 'interested' glance he'd received yesterday from Pandora Barrie, the famous authoress whose shower was faulty.

'Shame on you, Mitchell,' he murmured, striding purposefully to the end of the passage, then turning left towards Room 17, and within it, the lady who had literary pretensions.

Though it felt like a form of unfaithfulness, he had to admit Ms Barrie was attractive. He'd admired her slim, elfin figure when she'd arrived, and thought her dark, rounded eyes intriguing. The faintly dreamy expression she wore could've been inspired by the ever-present muse, he supposed, but a more likely cause was some sort of defect in her vision. He'd seen her fiddling for her spectacles as she was about to sign the register, and sympathised – although in his case the problem was relatively minor, and his glasses more cosmetic than functional.

But whatever was wrong with Pandora Barrie's eyes, it hadn't stopped her staring at him! She'd blushed very prettily when he'd smiled and taken her hand luggage, then blushed again, visibly quivering, when she'd given him his tip and their fingers had touched.

24

As he'd left, he'd wondered what she wrote about, and later he'd quizzed Dani on the subject.

'I don't really know. Love stories, I suppose . . .' she'd said, her expression wary, as if she'd suspected his motives in asking. 'I've never actually read any of her books.'

Cassie, his favourite chambermaid, had been far more helpful . . .

'Yuk! Awful stuff! Sugar-sweet romances. No bonking . . . I wouldn't touch them with a bargepole.'

That he could believe, and he smiled, thinking of all the things that Cass *was* prepared to touch. Or suck, or stroke, or take into her lush, gilded body.

But that was another story altogether, and not one for Ms Barrie's pristine pages.

Composing his face, he knocked on the door, then listened to the flurry of activity within. For someone so famous, and presumably so wealthy and well travelled, Pandora Barrie had struck him as rather naive. In particular, she'd seemed unsure of her womanhood; although as a writer of successful romances, he would have thought she'd be supremely feminine.

'Hello,' he said, when she opened the door, 'I understand you've got a problem with your shower?'

'Oh . . . er . . . yes,' said the authoress, peering at him timidly, her eyes wide, 'It doesn't seem to want to work . . . I turn it on and all it does is dribble and drip. I wonder if you could do something with it?' With that she stepped back into the room in a flutter of pink silk that swirled out around her legs as she moved.

Mitch found it difficult not to laugh as she led him through into the bathroom. He had to bite the inside of his lips, and dig his nails into the palms of his hands. In spite of her supposed imagination, Pandora Barrie had fallen prey to a standard cliché – the 'vamp welcomes help in flimsies' scenario. Her négligé was so slight it was almost non-existent, and at the front it plunged to her midriff. She was overperfumed too, her heavy, floral scent so violently intense and sensual he almost imagined he could see it as a mist.

The trouble was that her hackneyed ploy was working. As he followed her across the room, he could feel his libido stirring and his cock jumping, and he knew he had found his convenient 'other woman'. Pandora's clothing, perfumery and manner were too blatant for the signals to be otherwise.

But why does she so suddenly want me? he wondered, watching the sway of the writer's slim hips beneath the substanceless fabric of her robe. The sheer pink silk was like a vapour, and he'd put money on her being naked beneath it. His penis lurched in his trousers, an automatic, faithless reaction that was as disturbing as it was exciting. What would Dani think if she knew how swiftly his attentions could shift? She'd think he was an unprincipled, perfidious sex-fiend. And of course, she wouldn't be far wrong!

It's for a book! Goddamnit! That's what it is! he thought suddenly, his mind flipping back to Pandora and her screamingly unsubtle behaviour. She's researching a seduction scene for a novel, and I'm the poor stooge who's being seduced!

Out of the corner of his eye, he took a sideways peek at Ms Barrie as she struggled with the long flapping shower curtain, her helplessness affectedly Monroe-like.

26

She was very pretty, he decided as he leant forward and studied what looked like a perfectly functional shower control. With her floaty hair, her fey mannerisms and her gently pointed features, she wasn't a bit like Dani Stratton, but she had a sweet charm all of her own. Pandora's looks were more wraithlike, more vulnerable, but they attracted him far more than the exotic, experienced persona she was *trying* to project. There was something very soft about the way she moved and the gestures she made. A guileless-ness. A girlish quality. He remembered what Cass had said about 'sugary' books, and wondered if Ms Barrie was planning to change her genre. From dulcet romance to hard raunchy glitz.

'It's the dial,' she said, moving forward, almost brushing his arm with her breast. 'It won't seem to budge . . .' As she spoke, she reached into the shower stall and twisted the control knob – and suddenly, and quite contrary to her claims, it whirled round smoothly and freely – and water tumbled down on them both!

Pandora let out a shriek and waved her hands to try and fend off the heavy, drenching stream, while Mitch simply reached for the knob and turned it to 'off', finding no flaw in the mechanism as he did so.

They were both completely soaked. Mitch could feel his trousers and his saturated underwear clinging to his skin, and when he looked down he realised what that meant. The sodden black linen was graphically outlining his erection. He reached for a towel and swung it in front of him strategically, then used its corner to dry off his glasses. The downpour hadn't had any effect on his penis whatsoever; in fact it seemed even stiffer than before. He wondered if Pandora had noticed it, in the seconds before he'd grabbed for the towel.

The authoress was certainly studying him very closely now. Her sugar-pink mouth was slightly open and her face a little flushed around the cheekbones. A whole panoply of emotions seemed to be flooding visibly through her; a blend of confusion, fear, and an attempt at fierce concentration – as if she were desperately trying to remember something. As he watched, her lips began to move a little, like an actress's when working through a script.

My God, that's just what she is doing! Mitch thought as the light suddenly dawned. She's set this up, and now she's struggling with her lines. With the dialogue that triggers 'the clinch' . . .

He chose to play along. 'Perhaps you should get out of those wet things?' he said softly, injecting his voice with the same pure, velvet sensuality that had always done the trick in the past. With some care, he replaced his spectacles, turning his body to one side so his hard-on was a little less obvious.

'Er . . . yes . . . Yes!' Pandora answered breathily, her fingers plucking at her négligé where it clung to her breasts like a film. She seemed far more concerned with her own appearance than his, and he wondered if she'd even noticed his crotch.

This was the moment – in the blue movies – when the heroine either stripped off without turning a hair, or instead, reached for the hero and initiated sex. It was fairly evident that Pandora had planned to do either one or both of these, but at the point of no return she seemed to have lost her nerve. He watched her attempt a smile, then touch her hand to her dark dripping hair before sliding it downwards, over her throat and her chest. The gesture should have looked seductive, but instead, looked comical. Without thinking, Mitch cracked a broad smirk.

It was the worst thing he could possibly have done.

Pandora's face suddenly crumpled in distress. Her lower lip trembled, her lashes fluttered wildly, and with a whimper she burst into tears.

'Oh sod it! I can't do this!' she half-cried, half-wailed, rubbing her face with the sleeve of her robe, 'I'm not sexy . . . I can't seduce you . . . Oh God, what am I going to do now?'

Her passionate sobbing re-doubled, and curiously, Mitch's desire re-doubled with it. His usual preference was for strong, gutsy females like Dani or Cass, or even Lois; but somehow, this time, emotional fragility aroused him. Pandora's dewy tears made him want her – and at the same time, made him guilty as a rat for feeling that way.

Then, as he took her in his arms, another thought occurred . . .

They were both wet through. Was it that silly business with the water affecting him? He'd teased Dani mercilessly about the effects of the 'Hotel Aphrodisia' spring, but for his own part he'd dismissed it as nonsense. As he did anything he couldn't rationally explain.

'There there,' he murmured, grinning at the clichéd response, but this time hiding it carefully. As gently as he could he hustled Pandora through into the bedroom, pausing only to snatch up more towels on the way. One of these he spread out on the bed, then made the sniffling woman sit down. Taking a second towel, he rubbed briskly at her back, her shoulders and her hair. He felt reluctant to rub her more intimately; it seemed ill-judged in

29

the face of such misery.

He couldn't turn the wanting off though, and as he sat down beside her, still towelling her shoulders, his erection just wouldn't lie down. It was pushing upwards against the wet black cloth of his trousers, making a visible bulge. Swivelling half sideways on the bed, he made another hopeless effort to hide it.

'What is it, Ms Barrie?' he asked, stroking her more slowly now, enjoying her tremulous warmth and the way her slim shape seemed to yearn automatically towards him. She seemed mortified by her own inept attempts at seduction, but somehow, when she wasn't actively trying, the process was effortless. Mitch clamped down on his own powerful urges, on the driving, ungovernable need to push Pandora on to her back on the bed, then kiss her till she gasped out his name.

'It's too silly,' she mumbled, covering her face with her hands. 'You'll laugh . . . You'll think I'm sad . . .'

'I won't,' he promised, staring down at her body. The towel had slid away now, and the waterlogged silk of her négligé was outlining every nuance of her figure: especially her small, delicately conical breasts and the hard little nubs of her nipples.

'Tell me,' he urged, moving closer even though he knew it was risky with her minimal confidence.

'Well . . .' She looked up at him, her grey eyes moist, but surprisingly trusting. 'You know I'm a writer, don't you?'

He nodded.

'The thing is . . .' She took a deep breath and let it out in a sigh. 'I've always written very romantic books. You know the sort of thing . . . Very chaste and clean, everything ends at the bedroom door with a long row of dots . . .' She looked at him, then shrugged. 'All very boring to you, I suppose?'

'Your books are very popular, though, aren't they?' he offered non-commitally.

'They *were*. I was a top seller . . . But recently, sales have been falling off alarmingly, and now my publisher wants something far raunchier . . . No dots, and more "action", if you see what I mean?'

He nodded again, his own imagination teeming with 'action'.

'I've tried to write sex scenes, but they turn out wooden and all wrong. My editor says there's no conviction. No spark. No authenticity . . .'

She fell silent then, and Mitch held his breath. Pandora was a beautiful woman, sexually attractive in her own genteel sort of way – surely she had *some* personal experience she could write about? He gave her shoulders a little squeeze; he was at a loss what to say or do and it was a condition he disliked intensely.

'But how the devil can they be authentic?' she stormed, sobbing furiously again, 'I never *have* any bloody sex to write about!'

He considered saying 'there there' again but didn't think it wise. She was clearly very unhappy and he was as befuddled as he was aroused by her. She *was* a desirable woman, so how come she didn't have a love-life?

'I used to have a boyfriend . . . A few years ago . . .' she gulped, reaching out blindly. Mitch handed her a towel to wipe her face on. 'But he died, and it took me a long, long time to get over him . . . And when I did finally stop grieving, I'd

31

got out of the habit of wanting anybody. I just wrote and wrote and wrote. I didn't seem to need anything else.' She paused in her diatribe, and looked up at him, fighting for a self-mocking smile. 'Pathetic, isn't it?'

'No, it isn't,' he answered. 'I can understand how you might feel . . .' He couldn't, but it seemed kinder to lie. 'But what *I* can't understand is how the men all around you could allow it to happen.'

She blinked at him, her smoke-coloured eyes incredulous.

'You're a lovely woman, Pandora,' he said, taking the towel from her hands and wiping gently at her tear-smudged make-up, 'That you're lonely is a terrible waste.'

It was another of those movie moments – but this time from a lush, romantic drama. With a sense that the move was almost choreographed, Mitch abandoned the towel, then pulled off his glasses and dropped them on the bedside table. Leaning forward, he pressed his mouth reverently to Pandora's.

He felt her sigh beneath the kiss, her breath sweet and deliciously minty. Seeing a momentary image of Dani's censuring face, he laid his tongue against Pandora's quivering lips and pressed – decisively – for entrance.

Her mouth opened without protest, and as he tasted and nibbled and probed, their damp bodies moved closer together. She made a little noise in her throat as he put his arms around her and pushed her backwards, but it sounded suspiciously like a growl of encouragement. There was hunger in it, almost desperation, as if the long months of solitude and celibacy had sharpened her appetite like a blade.

Mitch lifted his face and looked down into hers. Her eyes were heavy, almost slumberous. 'Shall we give you a little something to write about?' he asked, taking a calculated gamble that she wouldn't be upset or offended.

Pandora's only answer was to reach for him, weave her fingers into his still-wet hair, and force him to continue the kiss.

4 Something to Write About . . .

AS THEIR MOUTHS duelled, Mitch felt Pandora's hands grabbing at his body. Groping him. She was feasting on the dish she hadn't tasted for years, but going at it all too quickly, and not giving herself time to enjoy it. Beneath him, her hips were circling and her pubis massaged him through their clothes. Mitch was confident of his power to contain himself, but stimulation like this was overwhelming, and he was still aroused from his encounter with Dani.

He tried to pull away, but Pandora seemed only to increase her efforts. She clung to his neck and shoulders like a wildcat, gasping into his mouth, her chest heaving with exertion, her thighs scissoring ceaselessly, her pelvis lifting and rubbing. Her nipples felt like pebbles against him and her whole body was burning with heat.

'Please . . . Please . . .' she whimpered, as he tore his mouth away, and gently cupped her chin. Her dainty face was flushed, and her eyes were dark, their pupils hugely dilated. There was a tiny smudge of lipstick at the corner of her mouth, and he blotted it gently with his finger, then wiped carelessly at his own lips too. Pandora moved again beneath him, and her arms closed tightly around his back.

'Take it easy . . .' he whispered, making his voice as gentle as he could. Her need was great, but her poise was fragile; she might feel rejection where it didn't exist. 'There's plenty of time. Let's take it slowly . . . You're so lovely and I want to enjoy you as much as you enjoy me . . .'

Her lips quivered for a second, and Mitch felt apprehension; but then she smiled, first doubtfully, then happily and he knew the greatest danger was past.

'Like I told you,' she said quietly, lying suddenly still in his arms, 'I'm out of practice . . . I've completely forgotten how to behave.'

'It'll soon come back to you,' he murmured into her ear, starting a slim trail of kisses on the side of her neck, then tracking across her jaw, throat and chest.

As his mouth reached her breasts, he could feel the dampness of her négligé against his chin, and still kissing, he began unfastening the flimsy upper part of it. In an instant he had her bosom bared, and felt a surge of real pleasure at the sight of it. Her breasts weren't large, but their shape was exquisite. They were like small, perfectly ripened fruits, crowned by nipples that were hard and dark and rosy. Instinct told him they'd be especially sensitive, and when he touched his fingertip to one tight crest, she shuddered as if he'd touched it to her vulva, then cried out and tossed her head from side to side.

Mitch was enchanted. He'd never had a woman who responded so strongly to something so simple. Pandora's small breasts were miraculous,

35

and as he caressed them he conceived an idea. He could tease her to the very heights of rapture with only this gentle stimulation . . . Prepare her with orgasms induced purely by the touching of her breasts . . . Stir her senses to a knife-edge of madness so the final act, when it came, was a hundred times more meaningful and intense.

His cock was aching furiously now, but he steeled his every nerve to ignore it. There was a long, long way to go before he'd find his ease in this pretty woman's body, and it was down to him to set a slow, easy pace . . .

Pandora Barrie looked up into the handsome face above her, and wondered what on earth she was doing.

The man was a stranger; she barely even knew his name. She'd heard the confident-looking girl behind the desk call him 'Mitch', but that was all she knew about him. He was a combination of a reception clerk, porter and handyman, and not even part of the management; and here she was, lying soaking wet on a bed with him, while he stroked her naked white breasts. She felt happier than she had in a long time. . .

Pandora had always had tender, responsive nipples, but rarely had she had them touched with such inventive and consummate kindness. He was toying with her ever-so-lightly, switching from one little bud to the other with a devastatingly tantalising playfulness that sent bolts of pleasure darting swiftly through her body.

But some parts were getting more bolts than others, she realised deliriously, her thighs and hips weaving like a dancer's. And as Mitch very gently pinched her nipple it felt as if he were doing the self-same thing to her clitoris. Exerting the most subtle combination of pull and pressure, drawing the tiny bead away from her body and toying with it wickedly to please her.

She wanted to scream, but Mitch anticipated her, bringing his mouth down excitingly on hers. His tongue flipped insolently at hers, and she imagined it doing something similar in other places – dabbing at her breasts or her vulva. The thought made her burn for the deed, and she moaned low and hungrily in her throat, still unable to cry out or speak for the pressure of Mitch's lips on hers.

He kissed her for what seemed like an age, his fingers still massaging her breasts, their magic unhindered by her wrigglings. The more he touched her there, the more it seemed to act upon her sex. Between her legs, beneath her robe, she could feel herself swelling and widening, and her juices flowing out in a stream. If her négligé hadn't been soaked already, there would have been a damp spot beneath her bottom, she was sure. As it was the air was heavy with her odour, a rich, aroused scent that was so pungent it embarrassed her to smell it.

Could *he* smell her? she wondered, blushing deeply because she knew it was likely.

It didn't seem to put him off though. He was kissing her harder than before now, and his touch was getting fiercer at her breasts. He'd rolled somehow, and he was lying half across her, his strong body pressed firmly against her weaker one, and his hardness jabbing just where she was softest. He *did* want her. She knew it, and he couldn't hide it; but she sensed he was holding himself back.

How lucky I am! she thought, both her heart

and her sex leaping wildly as his mouth began another downward swoop. I could easily have picked someone else to do this. Some selfish, egotistical bastard. Some cold-hearted, self-centred stud with only his own satisfaction in mind.

Warm lips were at work on the slope of her breast now, and between them a cheeky tongue flickered. Pandora wasn't sure she could endure the pleasure of being properly licked just yet; her nipples felt like plum stones already, and the whole of her body was a trigger. She'd waited so long to come in from the wilderness that she knew her first climax would stun her. The very instant that Mitch kissed her nipple . . .

Looking down at her lover's sleek, squeaky clean hair, Pandora felt a rush of affection. For a moment she felt all weepy and maternal, then almost immediately, before she could register what was happening, the wonderful thing happened – the wonderful so-wanted thing – and a hot mouth fixed lightly on her teat.

She came immediately, shrieking like a banshee, astonished she could have forgotten such sweetness. Orgasm was a fiery red torrent inside her – implosion and explosion both – a sensation that strayed close to the unbearable and hit her system like a mind-bending drug. She was vaguely aware that she couldn't stop shouting, and that her guttural joy-filled yells were slaved to the pulsing of her body and the steady even sucks at her breast. She was thrashing like a lunatic and screaming just as madly, but Mitch's lips didn't waver for a second. His soft mouth continued to tug on her, and his mobile tongue darted and lapped.

Pandora wasn't quite sure when the climax

finished; it simply seemed to fade to a glow. Mitch stopped sucking at precisely the moment she wanted him to, and when he looked up from her body, he gave her the most cherubic, ingenuous grin, an expression that achieved the impossible, and made her want him even more than before.

Pandora moaned as her vulva rippled softly, and inside her an empty void yawned. This man on her bed had everything she needed; this handsome young man with his perfect white smile, and his thick dark hair that'd now flopped endearingly forward. And the empty place ached ever harder, as with an elegant almost throwaway gesture, he reached up and flicked the dangling black love-lick out of his eyes.

'You were ready for that, weren't you?' he observed, without a trace of mockery or humour. Kissing her just once, between her breasts, he began shuffling his body slightly on the bed, so he could lie full length alongside her.

Given time I could probably love him, thought Pandora detachedly as she watched Mitch neatly unfasten his tie, and then start on the buttons of his shirt. He was worthy of love, she decided, both for his superb, male beauty *and* for his sexual sensitivity. You couldn't ask for a better mix of the two.

And yet she wasn't sure if *she* was the woman to love him ... She was ready for lovemaking, yes, but for the emotion itself? Well, perhaps not yet ... She needed life to be simple at the moment, so she could write her new novel. A prospect that was suddenly enticing, and seemed well within the scope of her powers ...

As Mitch bared his muscular torso, Pandora prepared a description. Something she could use, later, when she could think more clearly and clinically. The man before her would make an irresistible literary hero, she realised, and just hoped she could do him full justice.

Touching his skin, she tried to conjure up the words. Silky. Satiny. Immaculate. They were all expressive, but none of them quite caught the marvellous finesse of his flesh, and its superior resilience and smoothness.

When he began unfastening his belt – and then his trousers – all language slid away like running water and feelings rushed in and took its place. He wore the plainest of plain white jockey shorts, and as they were still thoroughly soaked from the shower, they revealed a lot more than they hid. Pandora could see his penis perfectly through them; every nuance, every contour, every vein.

Sensing her mood, and apparently relishing her scrutiny, Mitch took her shaking hand and pressed it to him.

He was hot beneath the thin wet fabric, and throbbing very slightly in her fingers. Pandora was awed by his size, but again felt that strange sense of nurturing. It was downright weird to feel motherly about a man's erection, but she supposed it was because a cock was also so vulnerable. It was the very essence of what made him a man, yet at the same time it was defenceless against an impact or a blow. Or even a disparaging, cruelly meant word.

You're going doolally, Barrie, she thought, quite amazed by her odd mental wanderings. Feeling another soft pulsation against her fingertips, she focused herself purely on the pleasurable side of the equation, and the prospect of Mitch's hardness deep inside her.

'Uncover me,' he gasped, his voice no longer

quite even. Pandora's trembling hands fumbled and she cursed inwardly. It seemed an age before the shorts slid down freely, and the flesh they contained jutted out.

Again, she considered herself lucky. Mitch's penis was so thick and stiff and vibrant it seemed to call out to *her* sex like a magnet. She wanted to straddle him, to enclose him and ride him to oblivion and beyond. His very size alone should have intimidated her, and yet instead it seemed to fill her with confidence. Feeling wanton, and suddenly powerful, she reached out and touched him, enjoying the way he grunted expressively as her fingertip traced the shape of his glans.

'Oh God, please,' he panted, as the tables turned and Pandora loosened the ties of her robe.

The pink silk confection came apart effortlessly, but she would have destroyed two hundred pounds' worth of Janet Reger's finest just to make herself naked for Mitch. With a grand and carefree abandon, she flung the flimsy thing across the room.

Mitch wasn't naked but that didn't matter. There was something deliciously decadent about him lying there with his shirt undone and his penis poking out of his trousers. When he made as if to get up and strip off, Pandora pressed her hand down on his chest, and then, with a grace she'd forgotten she possessed, she flung a leg astride his hips and made ready.

When his glans touched her groove she almost came. It took a huge effort of will not to, but she bit her lip, took a breath, and rode the spasms. Slowly, oh-so-slowly, she let her weight carry her down, moving and adjusting instinctively so his flesh could reach her very deepest parts.

'Oh yes!' she cooed, her response automatic

41

and joyous. It seemed so natural to be filled by a man again, and feel her inner walls stretched by his girth. As Mitch thrust upwards, the force of it pulled hard on her clitoris, and the tension was a delight in itself. She felt his fingers reach intuitively for her – then connect with both her breast *and* that tiny quivering button in the very same magical instant.

She'd tried to hold back, but she couldn't any more. Just as she had when he'd sucked her nipple, she climaxed instantaneously and cried out, her voice cracking and wavering with happiness.

Her bliss was dark and sweet, pouring over her like a heavenly syrup that pooled in the basin of her loins. Seconds later, and keening with pleasure, she felt Mitch's hot flesh leap inside her as he added his own shouts to the mêlée.

It was a sensation beyond words. Something that couldn't ever be quantified verbally. But as she fell forward across her lover's heaving chest, and listened to his harsh, broken gasps, Pandora knew that very soon she'd be attempting the impossible . . .

I wonder if I should be insulted? pondered Mitch, as he walked slowly along the landing, struggling in vain with his tie's soggy knot.

Women he'd made love to were usually quite affected by the process, and he often left them sleeping contentedly. Pandora Barrie, however, had leapt up off her bed immediately, and was even now tapping away industriously at her laptop. Mitch supposed it was a compliment of sorts, and that he'd inspired her, but something macho in his ego was annoyed.

Women! he thought, knowing even as he

thought it that he was behaving like a stereotypical stud, yet feeling helpless in the grip of his conditioning.

Staring down at himself, he saw a total saturated mess. His clothes, both under and outer, were disgustingly clammy against his skin and a swift trip to his room was in order – even though Dani would be fuming by now.

There were certain other things he had to do too, and as he thought of them, and her, he smiled. His sparring partner looked incredible when she was angry, almost as stunning as she did when aroused, although the two had a great deal in common. He thought of how pink and wild-eyed she'd been when he'd climbed out from under the desk this morning, and imagined her looking like that in bed, after he'd finished making love to her properly. He'd pleasure her so completely that she wouldn't have the breath to do a Pandora and jump up and start working straight away.

He grinned again. It'd be a tough job but someone had to do it! Whistling cheerfully, he strode towards his room.

The high-pitched whistle of the facsimile machine shook Dani rudely out of her reverie. She was sitting in the tiny office, just behind the reception desk, and in a confined space the fax noise was deafening.

Dani didn't make a habit of daydreaming in work's time, but this morning was a justified exception. The incident with Mitch had shaken her profoundly, and even though she'd had chance to slip away, get a glass of mineral water, and generally settle herself down, she could still feel his touch on her body.

And Mitch and his outrages weren't the only things on her mind.

Who was behind this MJK thing? she wondered. Was there really a spy in the hotel? And if so, the sixty-four-thousand-dollar question was . . . who was it? She frowned as she reached out to tear off the fax, mentally beginning to list the candidates, then let her lower jaw drop with astonishment when she saw what was on the printed flimsy paper.

It was headed by an elaborate but elegant logo comprised of three entwined letters: an 'm', a 'j' and a 'k'. This in itself was enough to set her hackles rising – but what made it more alarming than ever, was that the fax was addressed for *her* attention. To 'Dani' Stratton, not 'Daniella' or even 'Ms' Stratton . . .

Dear Dani, it began, *as you may or may not know, the Bouvier Manor Hotel has recently been acquired by my organisation. What you may or may not also know is that my policy is always to check out such acquisitions in person – for an unspecified period – before I make operational changes. This fax is what you might call a 'sporting' warning that the aforementioned surveillance has begun, and so far I've recorded not only a number of serious financial anomalies, but also instances of grossly inappropriate behaviour by supposedly trustworthy employees. Some rather 'dangerous liaisons' have been formed . . . Any thoughts on how all this might be handled?*

There was no signature.

'Oh shit!' whispered Dani, the curling fax shaking in her hand. 'Oh shit, oh shit, oh shit . . .'

Dropping the horrid missive on the desk, she smoothed it out, and tried to analyse what it meant. Although it was unsigned, the content was all 'me' and 'I' and 'my' . . . It wasn't from a characterless consortium, it was from one man, or perhaps one woman. The mysterious 'MJK'. The single all-powerful entity who was obviously watching them in person, rather than by means of some accountant or lackey. The new owner of the hotel was walking amongst them right now, she realised, probably in the guise of a newly arrived guest. Still trembling finely, she returned to the open reception desk and pored over the recent registrations.

Which of them had heard her called 'Dani'? She picked up a scrap of paper to jot down the likely candidates. Anyone who'd been around the desk area was a possible . . . Mitch, Cassie – her friend amongst the chambermaids – and various others on the staff always addressed her by her nickname, and any guest who was passing could easily have heard them.

Who'd just arrived and was particularly well off?

The first name Dani wrote was 'Pandora Barrie'. Despite a quiet period recently, the novelist had at one time frequently topped the best-seller lists and was reputedly a multi-millionairess. She also had a strangely watchful air about her, especially where Mitch was concerned.

That thought led to another which filled Dani with abject horror.

What the hell was Mitch doing now? She re-read the words 'grossly inappropriate behaviour' and 'dangerous liaisons'.

Oh God, had he made a pass at la Barrie? She was very attractive, and – of course – very rich. Dani didn't think Mitch was either stupid, or mercenary, but everyone had a weak moment sometime . . . and unfortunately his might be now. It seemed unlikely that a romantic novelist could also be a business tycoon, but the slightly cloak and dagger nature of the fax did suggest an imaginative mind.

There were other ways of thinking creatively though. The man who'd arrived just after Mitch's disgusting performance – Perry McFadden – was well known as an innovative 'noise' in big business. He was confident, wealthy, attractively into his fifties and wearing superbly well. Aware of his vast entrepreneurial success, Dani underlined his name and deemed him a prime suspect. He'd even – she'd gathered from the trade press – bought a hotel or two in the past . . .

Even so, this 'surveillance' thing was a sneaky way for an honest businessman to conduct himself, and Perry McFadden seemed very open and conventional. The arrival of the fax didn't seem to fit either, although Dani was well aware that there were methods of 'remote' communication. And she had seen Perry MacFadden's rather glamorous PA carrying a laptop computer.

But then again, Pandora Barrie had had a 'portable' in her luggage too. Everyone who was anyone had them nowadays – and if you combined one with a modem and various other trick-bits, you could probably send faxes from just about anywhere. Including a hotel bedroom!

Feeling increasingly agitated, but trying to stay calm, she added another name to the list.

Jamie Rivera.

Tennis was the man's first love, but he was reputed to be something of a shrewd investor too, with plenty of prize money and sponsorship earnings to plough into lucrative ventures. He also had an impish sense of humour, judging by his occasional comedic antics on the tennis court.

46

Spying on his own employees might just be his idea of fun.

Underneath Jamie Rivera, she pencilled in another 'possible'; the woman Lois had advised her to watch out for – Amy Lovingood, the wealthy and very worldly widow. Her being at the hotel with a toyboy didn't preclude the prospect of her combining a little business with her pleasure. It was the perfect cover, and Mrs Lovingood was another one who seemed suspiciously observant.

Mulling over her hit list, Dani wondered what the rest of the staff would think of the mysterious fax?

Richard would probably wet himself! she thought, smiling in spite of herself. Their hopelessly nefarious manager would be in the deepest trouble of all of them – mainly due to a number of unusual bills and invoices that Dani had seen passing through the accounts system lately. She'd debated at length with her conscience about mentioning what she knew, but in a way she felt quite sorry for Richard. He was weak and ineffectual, and led by the nose – and most probably by certain other parts – by the fearsome and implacable Lois. They were obviously in some kind of swindle together, but Dani had no doubt that the Ice Queen would drop her stooge without a second thought the instant discovery was imminent.

Studying the fax again, and then the list beside it, Dani tried to will that their proximity throw up some secret connection. A sign to guide her. But there was nothing . . . If only she had someone to talk it all over with. A friend, an ally she could trust.

The trouble was that free-wheeling Cass – the

one she felt most inclined to confide in – would only shrug, say 'a job was a job', and dismiss everything as the vagaries of 'the Goddess'. If everything fell around their ears, Cass would just jam her few belongings in her rucksack and bum around the country for a while. Beautiful half-Romany Cass had a loose association with convention at the best of times, and would probably end up back on the New Age trail, where she'd been before this, her latest stab at 'normal' life.

Dani thought fondly of her sweet, feckless friend, then frowned again, now thinking of someone who'd been far more intimate than her favourite 'traveller', but whom she wasn't quite sure she could even call a friend at all now.

Talk about 'dangerous liaisons' . . . Where the devil was Joseph Mitchell when you needed him?

5 Nowhere to Run

AT LUNCHTIME, WHEN Dani came off duty, Mitch still hadn't turned up.

'You bastard, where are you?' she muttered on the way to her room. She really wanted to talk things over with him and show him the fax, because in spite of his unspeakably disruptive behaviour, the man had common sense too. Mitch would see this latest development rationally, and might have a no-fuss solution to it too.

Unlocking her tiny room, Dani stepped inside and shrugged off her jacket, aware that the rigours of the morning had made her sweat beneath her arms and in her groin. Almost obsessively fastidious, she hated not being immaculate, and wrinkled her nose in disgust. She could smell primal, pheromonal perspiration, and another scent that came from lower down. The result of Mitch and his sly stimulation.

The logical thing to do was shower immediately, and she began gathering her things in readiness. But as she reached into a drawer for clean cotton undies, Dani felt a sudden heady surge of restlessness. She felt like running and running and running and expending huge amounts of energy and calories in an effort to clear her muddled mind.

'Run first, shower second,' she muttered, wriggling into her shorts and vest, then scrabbling beneath the bed for her trainers.

Just as she was doing up her laces, there was a knock at the door.

Mitch, you pig! she thought, as her senses revved up wildly. She looked around behind her at the narrow but serviceable bed, and imagined herself flat on her back, her legs wide open, being pleasured by Mitch's long penis. Goddamn the bastard! Even when he made her furious, she still wanted him. Wanted him so much she could kill him!

'Come in!' she called, her voice slightly croaky.

Her visitor was good-looking and desirable, but not Mitch.

'Coming for some scram?' enquired Cassandra Jenkins, one of the hotel's chambermaids and Dani's closest friend on the staff.

'No ... I don't think so ... I'm not very hungry.' Dani fumbled with her laces, struck – as ever – by the other woman's earthy, unaffected sexiness.

Cass was dark, exotic and voluptuous, with long, slightly slanted deep brown eyes and a jet black mane of dreadlocked hair that tumbled luxuriantly down across her shoulders and reached almost as far as her waist. Her body was rounded and curvy, and though her bosom was bigger and lusher than Dani's, on Cass the extra inches looked perfect.

As she often did with Cass, Dani felt both happy and confused. She loved having the beautiful, dark-eyed woman as her confidante, but with friendship came other more troubling emotions. Awe, a slight edge of fear, and an alarming degree of attraction.

'What's up, hon?' Unconsciously compounding the dilemma, Cass sat down and slid an arm around Dani's shoulders, smiling wryly when Dani started shaking, 'You've got something on your mind, haven't you? Come on, you can tell Auntie Cass.'

'It's *that*!' Dani pointed to the fax which lay on the dresser. Well, it was *partially* to blame . . .

'Oh Lor!' breathed Cass as she read. Flicking the paper with her forefinger, she narrowed her eyes and stared at it intensely. Her profound, almost seer-like concentration gave Dani a chance to recover.

'Who is it then?' Cass went on, 'One of the staff . . . or one of the guests?'

It had never occurred to Dani that the mole was on the staff. It was possible, but her instincts rejected the idea. 'It's one of the guests, I'm sure of it,' she said firmly. 'I've even made a shortlist.' With a deep breath she reeled off the names.

'So, Holmes . . . how do we go about it?' enquired Cass, her dark eyes sparkling.

As her best friend spoke, Dani recognised her own unconscious intentions. Personally, and professionally, she had an intense desire to discover the faxer's identity. And she wanted to unmask him – or her – before he – or she – got around to doing it.

'I don't know . . . But we'll find a way!'

'Well, *I* think better on a full stomach.' Cass rubbed her belly and grinned. 'Are you sure you won't eat? It'll only be the usual staff slop . . . but in a dire situation like this we've got to keep the engines well stoked.'

'No, I'll pass . . . *I* think better when I'm

51

running. Why don't you come with me for a change?'

Cass had laughed then, laughed so heartily that her beautiful, bra-less breasts had swayed in her cheesecloth bodice. Dani could well imagine that her friend was still chuckling now, and tucking into a lunch to make a weightwatcher blanch. Every one of Cass's appetites was prodigious . . .

As if I haven't got enough trouble! thought Dani as she ran through the woods, wishing she could face up to her feelings. There was a reckoning coming with both Cass and Mitch, and just when she needed as few distractions as possible. She needed her brain to be sharp, and unfuddled by the demands of her body. Increasing her speed again, she tore along the track like a sprinter, trying to erase her lustful meanderings and concentrate on the matter in hand.

The problem was that the subterfuge itself was sexy. The idea of a secret observer aroused Dani. It seemed bizarre, but as she thought about this sender of cryptic, threatening faxes, she felt something in her lower belly quicken and the groove between her legs grow moist. Man or woman, it didn't seem to matter which it was . . .

Who are you? she cried silently, but got no answers from the trees to either side.

Perry McFadden – the one she most suspected – was distinguished and handsome, and she imagined him dominant in both bedroom and boardroom. She'd not seen a lot of his body, but he'd looked lean and strong in his Savile Row suit, full of stamina and the ability to perform. He'd be determined and tenacious and long-lasting and give climax after climax after climax.

The other male possibility was Jamie Rivera – an athlete, no less! A man whose physique was well-known to television tennis viewers all over the world, because he had a showman's habit of taking his shirt off and flinging it to the crowd, and wearing shorts that were soft and ultra-thin. It didn't require much imagination to picture that chunky, muscular body naked, then extrapolate how it might function in bed.

Her two other suspects were women, and Dani tried hard not to dwell on just how much *they* attracted her too . . .

Oh God! No matter how fast and far she ran, there was no hiding place. No way to stop dwelling on sex. And longing for it! She was acutely turned on as she sped along the path; her breasts tense and aching as they bounced to the rhythm of her stride. Down between her legs she was wet through yet again, and her labia were enlarged and tender.

Faltering, she considering stopping to masturbate – so she could think straight again. Slowing to a halt, she looked back along the path . . .

The Bouvier Woods were dense with mature trees whose branches made a canopy above her. The track she was on was the only clearly marked route through the woodlands, and from where she stood she could no longer see the open park she'd left behind. She was deep in the heart of an enchanted forest, and completely and utterly alone. She could satisfy her torments in peace, with no-one around to observe her secret pleasure. Playing safe, though, she decided to go on a little farther down the track.

If I wasn't such a stubborn bitch, I could've had company for this, she thought resignedly as she walked. Either Mitch or Cass would've been happy to help me . . . Far more than happy.

Suddenly, Dani heard the sound of faint conversation, and realised she wasn't alone after all. There was someone on the path up ahead. She could hear a male voice, and a female one, both talking softly but still uncannily audible in the peculiar acoustics of the woods. Light-footed in her rubber-soled trainers, she moved stealthily forward.

The voices seemed to come from amongst the trees to her right, and after a few moments of tiptoeing gingerly through bushes and bracken, she came upon a small, sunken clearing.

The little hollow was lit like a film set, the midday sun shining beneficently down from above, but a little filtered by the foliage of the trees all around. Settling down noiselessly on her knees, hidden by a convenient clump of undergrowth, Dani studied the occupants of the dip: a man and a woman, embracing.

She recognised them immediately. The woman was Mrs Amy Lovingood, the amazingly rich widow, and the man was her toyboy, the gorgeous young Ross Frazetti. Both of them were already half undressed, and as they kissed, and fondled each other's part-clad bodies, Dani gnawed her lip in frustration. Already feeling desperate for release, she'd only gone and stumbled on a scene that was guaranteed to arouse her even more!

Rolling on the forest floor, Mrs Lovingood was no longer the cultured sophisticate Dani had admired in Reception. The Jean Muir suit was gone, as were the Maud Frizzon shoes. Her denims were probably a designer label, but they were flung willy-nilly across a bush. The woman was still wearing her white, pure silk shirt, but it was unfastened at the front, rucked and crumped, and adorned with long smears of dark earth. Her grey lace bra was half-twisted around her body, and her breasts were almost totally exposed.

The lovely Ross had lost most of his clothes too. His jeans were strewn across the greenery with his mistress's, as were his socks, his shirt and his briefs. The only thing he still wore was a white racer-back vest, which contrasted like a dream with his tawny-brown bottom where it gleamed smooth and naked in the sunlight.

The sight was so erotic that Dani had to stifle a moan. The contrast of the refined, pale-skinned woman and the swarthy Italianate youth was electrifying, as was the way they shimmied and groped at each other. Dani felt a sudden craving to *be* Mrs Lovingood, to be lying there on the damp forest floor with a lusty young cock pressed against her, just begging to be buried in her body. And as the other woman groaned 'Yes, Ross! Yes!', Dani couldn't hold out any longer. With a silent cry of her own, she pressed a hand to the juncture of her thighs and rubbed her sex through her thin satin shorts.

Massaging cautiously, afraid of a noisy orgasm, she kept her gaze locked on the slowly writhing bodies. Mrs Lovingood's legs were wide open and she seemed to be taunting young Ross without mercy by massaging her loins against his crotch. Dani was astounded he could contain himself so well, and not ejaculate on his teasing lover's belly. She could see his buttocks tensing convulsively, as if he were taking a test of endurance not performing a sweet act of love.

'Oh Ross, you feel incredible,' Amy Lovingood murmured, reaching up to caress his boyish black curls. 'You're so big . . . So ready . . . I could come just like this . . .' Wriggling beneath him, she made an uncouth grunting sound that Dani recognised from her own experience as being the immediate precursor to a climax. 'Ooh . . . Yes! I can feel you right up against my clit . . . Oh God, yes, that's it . . . Oh God! Oh Jesus! Oh yes, love, I'm coming! I'm coming! I'm coming!' Mrs Lovingood's legs flailed and kicked wildly in time to her litany of clichés, and with her free hand she clawed at Ross's bottom.

It was orgasm that seemed to last an age, and Dani felt her own sex quivering in empathy. She wasn't coming, but she was barely a breath away from it. Her finger rocked lightly on her clitoris, buffered only by her shorts and her panties. She was frantic to climax, but if she did, she'd cry out . . . and the lovers in the hollow would hear her.

Being caught 'peeping' could mean disaster, regardless of whether Amy Lovingood owned the Bouvier Manor or not. Paying guests had a right to do whatever they wanted in the hotel's private grounds, and to be found spying on them would probably result in a dismissal . . .

Even more than this, Dani wanted to remain undiscovered so she could see what happened next. The extreme tautness of Ross's brown rump told her he was as close to the edge as she was. His muscles shone like finely polished wood, and she wondered how much longer he could stay erect against his lover's pulsing sex. Surely, in the glow of her own satisfaction, Mrs Lovingood would allow him to take her?

Contradicting her desire to stay hidden, Dani began picturing a scene in which she sprang from her niche in the bushes and joined in the vivid tableau before her. She imagined herself splitting her thighs as wide as Mrs Lovingood's, then rubbing her vulva on Ross's firm bottom. His flesh would be red hot against her, a rock of male muscle on which to beat her agonised clitoris. As she came, she'd reach beneath him and fondle Mrs Lovingood too, dislodging that rich grey lace with her fingers and exploring those well-bred white curves.

In the real hollow scene, Mrs Lovingood purred throatily and started pushing against Ross's prone body. Dani's heart began to pound, and without thinking, she flexed her thighs and made ready to rise . . .

But before she could move as much as an inch, she felt an arm like an iron band snake smoothly around her waist, and a large hand cover her mouth.

The shock was so immense she almost wet herself – and she wasn't quite sure that she hadn't actually done it – but even so, some instinct of preservation kept her silent. Her captor's hold was strong, and his cologne so familiar she could have screamed; so when he permitted her to turn a little way sideways, his identity was no real surprise.

Mitch! The swine! He was grinning down at her, his eyes brown and wicked behind his glasses . . .

Dani had never felt a more conflicting set of emotions in her life. She was turned on and frantic to have sex of any kind, yet at the same time she had a profound urge to murder Joseph Mitchell. She was being torn a dozen different ways, and only feet away, a beautiful scene of romantic eroticism was moving into a marvellous new phase. Her mouth still covered, she felt herself being lifted and turned, so she could see the glade from a much better angle . . .

Dear Lord, he's going to watch with me!

The idea was appalling, but electrifying too. She was helpless in his arms, as powerless to control herself as she'd been this morning in Reception. Mitch had total command of her and she *had* to stay silent and still. She couldn't thrash her way free or protest, because if she did the lovers would hear her. She was in a cleft stick, and the only thing to do was enjoy it . . .

Mitch's body felt large and strong behind her, and against her bottom something hard twitched repeatedly. She wondered how long he'd been nearby. Was it the lovers who'd inspired his stiffness, or her, crouched in the bushes in her flimsy shorts with an expresion of pure lust on her face?

As she refocused her attention, Dani saw Ross levering himself gracefully up off his mistress. Moving with extreme care, the boy moved to one side, and as he did so, she saw his penis.

Lois had said Ross Frazetti was eighteen, but his sex was that of a man who was mature and magnificently in his prime. His cock was substantial, but surprisingly elegant, with darkly swollen veins and a pretty, almost wandlike quality in spite of its girth and length. The glans looked almost irritated, its colour a deep rosy pink. Dani half hoped Mrs Lovingood would crouch down and take it in her mouth, but instead she leaned across and kissed his lips.

'What do you want, darling?' she asked indulgently, touching his flat brown belly, then laughing as his prick twitched and swayed.

In their hideout, Dani felt Mitch tighten his grip, and push his penis into the groove of her bottom. His lips moved moistly on the side of her neck, and more from the movement of his mouth than anything, she realised he'd whispered

'Lucky devil!'

Back in the glade, Ross Frazetti was blushing. His soft, red mouth worked nervously for a moment, then he slid close to Mrs Lovingood and murmured a few words in her ear. Dani was charmed by his bashfulness, and it was clear that Mrs Lovingood felt the same.

'Of course, my dear,' she said, smiling knowingly, then slid her thumbs beneath the straps of her bra. With a quick, deft movement, she flipped them off her shoulders and peeled down the cups completely, setting free her fine, pointed breasts. That the bra still encircled her midriff made her bosom look ten times more naked – the dark, sophisticated lace a foil for her creamy white flesh. With a trembling hand, Ross reached out and stroked one hard, peachy nipple. Mrs Lovingood sighed with approval, and while he fingered each puckered crest in turn, she slid her hands to the elastic of her knickers and skinned them down as she had done her bra. When they reached her knees, she just left them there, a bridge between her lewdly parted thighs. Her mound was a soft, glossy brown, the curls already glistening and sticky.

Without hesitation now, Ross made his fingers into a wedge and plunged them in, caressing his mistress quite roughly. Mrs Lovingood cooed heated encouragements, first lifting and flaunting her pelvis, then unexpectedly knocking away his hands.

'It's your turn, baby,' she said, rolling her slender body sideways, then coming up in an all fours crouch. Her haunches were raised for his inspection, offered – like a bitch's – to her mate.

Amy Lovingood's buttocks were as tight and rounded and toned as those of a girl in her teens.

Groaning almost in pain, Ross rose to his knees and took up a position behind her. His angelic face was strained with the effort of containing himself, and as Mrs Lovingood reached backwards to guide him, he bit deep into his fleshy lower lip. Pushing forward, he slid his cock inside her, then almost fell across her back, gasping and sobbing like a baby and covering her shoulders with a mantle of kisses.

For a moment, Dani thought the boy had climaxed, then she watched in awe as – yet again – he mastered himself, and began to thrust in smoothly and evenly. Mrs Lovingood, however, had no such control, and her shouts were frenzied and obscene. Ramming herself backwards against him, she took her weight on one elbow, and with her free hand rummaged crudely at her sex.

Ross seemed still to be trying to resist, but Mrs Lovingood was obviously too much for him. His fine, almost classical features contorted, then he started crying out too, yelling and shouting in triumph as quite plainly he orgasmed inside her.

Dani was happy for the couple in the clearing, and grateful for the hubbub they created. She couldn't keep her own gasps in now, or curb the wild thrasting of her limbs. Panting like a bellows, and moaning softly, she bit the hand that was clapped across her mouth . . .

She *had* to bite his hand or her moans would have turned into screams . . . Because without any warning, Mitch had shifted his position and his *other* hand had slid inside her shorts.

6   You Show Me Yours

THE TEMPTATION TO make noise was enormous, but drawing on the same reserves she had done earlier Dani managed to resist it. Twisting and turning like an eel on a hook, she mimed 'you bastard!' against Mitch's gagging hand.

In return, she felt a movement inside her panties, then his fingers settled masterfully on her clitoris. To compound the felony, he released his sure hold on her face, and left it solely up to her to keep quiet.

Dani felt herself colouring furiously, embarrassed by her body's helpless wrigglings, and by the moisture that bathed her whole sex.

The two of them were lying more or less full length on the forest floor now, peering through a thin, scrappy bush, with their heads towards the couple in the hollow. Mrs Lovingood and Ross were still crying and moaning with pleasure, but their voices had mellowed and gentled, as if they'd descended from the very highest peak and found a quieter, more pacific plateau. Distracted, Dani could barely focus on them, but when she did, she saw Ross's tanned thighs tautly quivering, the corded muscles tensed-up with the

61

obvious effort of *not* collapsing down on to his mistress. The boy wasn't more than twenty, Dani guessed, but he had the makings of a superlative lover. Even in the highest throes of passion, he seemed always to put his partner's needs first.

Unlike some people! she thought angrily, squirming in the two-fold trap of both Mitch's grip and their strange situation. As the couple in the glade fell silent, the constraints on their watchers increased; something Mitch used to his advantage as his efforts between her legs grew more diligent.

Dani bit her lip hard, and felt tears of strain in her eyes. Mitch's finger was circling her clitoris now, and in time to it, he was grinding his cock into her bottom. A few thin layers of cloth kept his flesh from hers, but even so she could feel his hard heat. The shape of his fat, bulging glans was as clear as life as it rocked in her tender anal groove. The muscles of her thighs began to twitch and contract just as Ross's had done, and her vulva fluttered and pulsed. She was right on the edge of an orgasm, and she knew she couldn't stay silent much longer. There was blood in her mouth already, where her sharp teeth had gouged at her lip.

Then, just as she thought she couldn't bear a second more, the flickering finger withdrew. And the torture increased. *Not* coming was far worse than coming ... and her sex was so wet and engorged now that she felt the beginnings of a moan of desperation.

But Mitch had anticipated her. His hand, still pungent from her sex, closed gently across her face and contained the ragged cry at its birth. Dani felt tears streaming down her face, tears of unbearable frustration. In that moment, she hated the man against her with every fibre of her being, but would've fallen on her knees and begged him if he'd offered her the merest crumb of release. Her shame and debasement were total.

Or at least they seemed so, until Mitch shifted his weight, modified his hold on her, and took one of her stiff, swollen nipples in a pinch between his finger and thumb. Mouthing her name against her ear, he began twisting lightly at the tip of her breast, rolling it this way and that, then pulling it outwards and away from her body. Dani wanted – needed! – to scream, but the hand across her mouth tightened firmly. Her pelvis beat to and fro, as if it were trying to create stimulation out of simple momentum; but as her movements threatened to become noisy, Mitch rolled his body yet again, and squashed her thrashing form close against the turf.

They lay like this, with Dani's sex aching and throbbing, for what seemed like an eternity. Every now and again Mitch would delicately tweak her nipple – to keep her on the boil – and Dani could do nothing but watch, through bleary eyes, as the pair in the hollow settled back into the realm of normality.

Disentangling their relaxed bodies, Mrs Lovingood and Ross picked grass stalks off each other, and fumblingly re-arranged each other's clothing, whilst still exchanging endearments and kisses.

Despite her perilous situation, Dani was impressed once again by Ross. He seemed to cherish his much older mistress, and adore her without a trace of reservation. His every action was gentle, his every look worshipful yet not in the slightest way sickly.

He loves her, thought Dani, then caught her

breath as Mitch's fingers nipped her teat. The contrast between the respectful Ross and the hateful swine who was molesting her made her furious; but to her horror, she felt even more excited. Fresh juices slickened her folds, and her nipple seemed to burn in Mitch's grip. Her hips leapt, and the resulting small sound made Mrs Lovingood look round, her smooth brow crumpling with disquiet.

Dani held her breath, and tried to stay still, even though Mitch continued to roll and tug and plague her, but fortunately Ross Frazetti chose that moment to take his mistress back into his arms for a long and very passionate kiss. The couple were standing now, and the matching heights of their contiguous, embracing bodies made a harmonious and beautiful sight.

The kiss went on for an age, and looked thorough. Dani almost thought they might start to make love again, but eventually Ross stepped back, trailed his fingers over Mrs Lovingood's face, then bent down to reach for her black cashmere cardigan, the last remaining item of her clothing. This he helped her into, and buttoned solicitously, whilst murmuring something rueful about the mud-stained condition of her blouse. Mrs Lovingood answered by touching his glowing face, then slinging an affectionate arm around his waist. Still talking softly, the two of them then began walking back towards the main track.

'Mitchell, I'll kill you!' hissed Dani, as soon as she dared.

The threat was real and honestly felt, but a split-second after she'd uttered it, Dani smiled. This was the second extravagant promise of homicide today, and its foolishness amused her immensely.

'Ssssh,' murmured Mitch in her ear, then surprisingly, he released her from his grip.

Shimmying away from him, Dani's every instinct was to jump up and run like the wind; but instead, the devil that dwelt inside her made her stay exactly where she was. She sat up and fixed her gaze on Mitch. Yes, she'd stay, and beat this handsome, brown-eyed beast at his own disgusting game.

Mitch was wearing a black satin vest and shorts – much like her own red ones – and as he scooted himself up into a sitting position, his erection bulged hugely against the fabric at his groin. To Dani's satisfaction there was also a thin sheen of sweat on his face. He was as flustered as she was, she realised, and instead of the look of infuriating complacency on his face – which she knew would've enraged her – she saw wonder and a sudden, strange confusion. He was looking at her intently and almost warily, as a snake might look at a mongoose.

'Y . . . your eyes . . .' he stammered, his gaze level and focused.

As her contacts were only for camouflage, Dani often didn't wear them when she was alone, to let her eyes rest. Just before she'd left her room, she'd slipped out the two tiny circles of dark blue glass and left them soaking in their pot of cleansing fluid.

'So laugh then!' she said defiantly. 'I know I'm a huge source of amusement to you, so these must be an absolute scream.' She gestured towards her face, and her unusual, mismatched irises.

'They're fascinating,' he whispered, sounding genuinely awed. 'They're not funny at all . . . They're beautiful.' He moved closer, and it took every effort on Dani's part not to retreat. His maleness was raw and potent, and she couldn't discount his perverse sense of humour. Any second now he might strike out and grab her, then inflict some brand new indignity.

But he didn't. All he did was touch her face very gently, like a butterfly alighting on her temple, and stare fixedly into the eyes that intrigued him.

Mitch's eyes were equally fascinating to Dani. Behind his glasses they glowed like dark, amber jewels. There was currently no sign of lust in them, just a profoundly hypnotic concentration. An expression that affected Dani as much as, if not more than desire would have done.

'Never mind my eyes!' she cried in exasperation. 'Let's turn our attention to other parts, shall we?'

'Gladly,' purred Mitch, his cheekiness back with a vengeance. 'Which particular ones were you thinking of?'

'Shut up.' Dani kept her voice soft and cool, knowing how much he loved seeing her rattled. 'What I'd like is an explanation of why you keep interfering with me.'

Mitch seemed to consider this a totally routine question. He shrugged expressively, then with a flagrant insolence and crudity, reached down and put his hand on his crotch.

'It's because you're beautiful, and I want you,' he said simply, his hand moving slightly as he spoke.

'Well, you're not bloody well having me!' growled Dani, aware that she was losing it, and far too soon after she'd decided she wouldn't.

'But why not?' Mitch persisted, '*You* want *me*.'

Dani took several deep, centring breaths. She

was in danger of throwing away any advantage she'd ever had.

'What I want—' she said very precisely, '—is an orgasm, Mitch, not you.'

'Then have one.' Mitch's eyelids drooped behind the glinting lenses of his glasses, and his whole expression became arch and sultry.

'Not while you're here,' replied Dani, 'I've had enough of indulging *your* perverted tastes . . .'

Mitch said nothing, but rolled his hips slowly and sleazily.

It would've been useful to say she found him repellent, but she didn't. He was one of the sexiest, most desirable men she'd ever met, and his wicked ways only increased his allure. As Dani considered this, a piquant idea occurred to her; something she knew she ought to dismiss out of hand, yet which felt more irresistible as every second passed.

'Well, if you won't leave me in peace, you can at least join in . . .'

'I'd be delighted,' he drawled, squeezing himself, then grimacing suggestively. 'You show me yours, Dani, and I'll show you mine . . . Deal?'

Dani couldn't help but laugh. It sounded naughty and juvenile, and she knew he'd *meant* it to sound that way. They were suddenly transported back to being two grubby, inquisitive kids, hiding out away from the adults and gleefully exploring their own bodies. It was so preposterous she couldn't say no.

'Deal,' she said, suppressing a snigger as she thought of last night's fantasy. Had she estimated his 'dimensions' correctly? 'But you first . . . You owe me one.'

'Ah, sweet Dani! Just say the word and I'll give you one.'

'Mitch!'

67

'All right already,' he murmured resignedly, 'Your wish is my command.'

As Dani watched closely, Mitch slid his thumbs into the waistband of his shorts, and with a shuffle, peeled them down to his knees. Leaning back against the stump of a tree, he struck what could only be called a deliberately exhibitionist pose, and rocked his hips to make his prick sway.

And there was plenty of it to sway. Dani licked her suddenly dry lips. She'd definitely been *under*estimating, rather than over. She'd been impressed by Ross Frazetti, a few minutes ago, but Mitch was markedly bigger, in girth as well as length. His penis was a darkly appetising club, rearing up straight and true from his groin and already slickly juicy at its tip. Completely mesmerised, Dani had forgotten her reciprocating pledge.

Mitch reminded her.

'Now you,' he said softly, as his long, graceful fingers drifted inevitably downwards.

With much trepidation, and an equal amount of titillation, Dani began tugging at *her* shorts. As they slid down her hips and thighs, they brought her panties off with them, the whole lot an inelegant bunch that tangled around her trainer-clad feet and for several seconds refused to come off.

When she'd finally worked herself free, Dani flung the cotton and satin bundle to one side, along with the irritating trainers, then settled down into a more comfortable position. Or as comfortable as she could be with her bare bottom on a grassy forest floor. She was naked from her waist to her white sports socks, and as she had no convenient tree to rest her back on, she bent one leg slightly – with knee up and foot flat down – to

68

give her body some balance and stability.

Dani was embarrassingly aware that her pussy was open and gaping, and that her pubis was glisteningly wet. Adjusting the angle of her hips, she half expected Mitch to make some comment, some insulting observation on how ready she was. She waited for the jibes, but instead he seemed lost in a fugue of enchantment. It was as if her sex had struck him to silence, even though he'd seen it and touched it this morning when he'd crouched beneath the desk and kissed her thighs.

He stayed quiet so long that Dani felt unnerved. She'd always been proud of her body, so much so that she'd even done some nude modelling . . . But now she had quivers of doubt. She'd let her pubic hair grow wild since her photo-spread days, and now she wondered if it looked too bushy. Perhaps Mitch didn't like women to be hairy down there? It seemed unlikely, because he'd been in seventh heaven this morning. Even so . . .

'You're beautiful, Dani,' he said suddenly, making her jump.

'You're not so bad yourself,' she quipped, knowing it was true. Mitch *was* one of the most impressively built men she'd ever seen, both sexually and in general physique . . . But how objective her assessment, she couldn't be sure. She'd exposed herself totally when she'd modelled, but then she'd been able to cut herself off from the people around her. Her detachment had been an invisible cloak around a deeper, inner nakedness, but with Mitch there was no such shield. She was involved, connected, and, whether she liked it or not, half bewitched by him – whether this morning, as a victim, or now as a willing volunteer.

'What did you think of the lovers?' she enquired,

seeking some, or any kind of comment that wouldn't sound evasive or banal.

Mitch looked thoughtful, then with his free hand – the one not clasped around his penis – he nudged his glasses up the bridge of his nose. Dani had seen him do this often when he was thinking, and when he smiled, she half dreaded his reply. Expecting the smile to widen to a sexy, teasing grin, she was surprised when he suddenly looked pensive.

'Mrs Lovingood is a very beautiful woman . . . and the young man seems to think a lot of her. He's graceful and generous, and she appreciates him . . .' He looked her straight in the eyes. 'They make a good couple, don't they?'

'Yes,' she answered quietly, thrown off balance by his seriousness.

'And what about us?' he said, his hand beginning to move on his stiff, reddened shaft, 'Do we make a good couple?'

'I . . . I don't know . . .'

'Let's see, shall we? His fingers slid faster and faster. 'Touch yourself, Dani. Let's share this properly . . .' His eyes looked almost black behind his glasses now, 'Please, Dani, please . . . Do it for *yourself*, if not for me.'

Moved by his plea, and more stirred than ever, Dani let her hand drop tentatively to her pubis.

As she touched herself, as her fingertip made contact with her clitoris, a small sound rose up through the greenery. A long, almost plaintive sigh of happiness.

A sigh that was Mitch's not hers . . .

At the sight of Dani caressing herself, Mitch's self-control wavered like a ripple through water. He'd thought himself totally in command of the moment, but it'd taken just one uniquely feminine gesture to undermine him, and without thinking he sighed in wonderment.

Dani had long, tapered fingers. Elegant fingers that curved like a pale benediction over the pinkness and slickness of her sex. As they flickered, probed, then dove in, Mitch felt his cock leap and surge. He'd never felt harder, never had an erection so solid; but at the same time, it felt dangerously precarious. If she did anything else, anything even the tiniest bit more erotic than she was already doing, he was scared he'd ejaculate in an instant. Just watching her first, tentative forays was killing him. If she began to rub in earnest, he was lost. Embarrassingly, ignominiously and adolescently lost. So much for his image as a stud.

Then, almost as if she'd read his thoughts, Dani shifted her position slightly and seemed to settle into a steady new rhythm. Her slender middle finger slid slowly back and forth in an action as old as time, and made Mitch nearly cry out in anguish. He'd seen women masturbate often enough, but somehow this simple, basic performance was the most exotic and sensuous ever.

The colour contrasts before him were mind-blowing; her red vest, her creamy-white belly, then the softer, more muted red of her thick pubic curls, and the vivid multi-pinks of her vulva. Her sex a living poem: swollen flesh, glossy hair and the thick silk of lush female fluids. It made his mouth water, his head spin and his cock ache furiously. The pleasure-pain was like none he'd ever known.

He remembered the feel of her sex against his fingers, and the smell of her luxuriant aroma. She was pungent now, he knew that, and

71

swimmingly moist. But there was a space between them, and air, and another smell: the delicate mossy freshness of the woodland. He thought of how it'd been when he'd crouched beneath her this morning, his face almost touching her crotch, so close he could almost have licked the flowing musk from her folds. He wished now – with all his heart – that he'd gone ahead and tasted her, so he could drown in the recollection of her flavour.

'Mitch . . . What's wrong?' she enquired quietly, her fingers stilling, and he realised his silence must seem strange.

'Just dreaming, Dani. Just dreaming,' he replied, hearing his own voice grow broken around the edges, made hoarse by his heavy, gasping breaths.

'What of?' she demanded, her fingers still working. She seemed lost in a fantasy of her own now, and he hoped with great passion *he* was in it.

'About you, this morning . . . What that feels like.' He nodded towards her belly, and her gently moving hand. 'The perfume of your body, and how you wriggled when I played with you . . .' He saw her odd eyes suddenly catch fire, so he raced onwards to prevent her getting angry. 'And last night . . . Last night in the bathroom. I remember your voice and the way you cried out . . . You were coming, weren't you?'

She didn't try to deny it, and admiration rushed through him like a wave.

'Yes, I was,' she answered, 'I felt horny so I gave myself pleasure . . . And I was cross, too. I thought it was that water you made me drink.' The fire had mellowed to mirth. 'Maybe it was . . . I don't know. Or maybe it's just you, you infuriating beast!'

They were at a pivotal moment. Mitch toyed – for a millisecond – with the idea of abandoning this ritualised show, and just asking, very humbly, if he could make love to her. But something, some instinct, told him that the ultimate joining could well bring them *too* close. Create an intimacy that the time wasn't ripe for. Not yet, at least . . .

On with the game then, he decided ruefully, gritting his teeth as his penis jerked wildly. Gasping again, he pinched it firmly – just beneath the glans – to contain the headlong rush of his semen.

'Okay . . . I am a beast . . . but I can't help it,' he apologised, panting. 'You excite me too much . . . I don't think I can last much longer! Oh God, please, Dani! Do the same things you were doing last night!'

'All right, I will!' Dani's voice had sharpened to a snarl, and as Mitch watched feverishly, she let her body fall backwards onto the grass, then straightened out her long, pale legs, and let her toes point directly towards him.

The foreshortened view was bizarrely erotic. Mitch stared straight into Dani's vulva, and watched the sunlight dance and glint on her juiciness, and the cords in her groin tense and flex. Her pose seemed perfectly designed for his convenience, and as she worked carefully with one narrow finger, almost nothing of the spectacle was hidden. He could see the dainty portal of her vagina, opening and closing like the mouth of an anemone; he could see her trim buttocks twitching, her anus small and fiercely tight, resisting the air as it'd resisted his intrusion this morning.

And when her bottom lifted off the ground, and she keened long and plaintively like a she-wolf, Mitch couldn't stop himself groaning too, or his body arching upwards like a bow. His penis was a rod of liquid fire in his fingers, connected by lightning to his brain and jetting pure white silk towards Dani.

The last thing he saw before he slumped against his tree was his come spattered thickly on her thigh.

Dani gazed up through the branches and saw a small patch of distant blue sky. She could feel grass beneath her buttocks and twigs poking into her, but somehow it didn't seem to matter. The whole area from her navel to her toe-tips was bathed in an afterglow of pleasure.

'Are you all right?' enquired a familiar voice, and though her conscience said she should leap up and put her clothes on, all her other parts were content to just lie. On display . . .

'Yes . . . I feel fabulous,' she replied dreamily, letting her fingers roam her belly and her thighs. Pausing, she explored a long patch of stickiness; something viscous, still warm, and not of *her* making.

'You look divine,' said Mitch, with genuine admiration and an endearing waver in his voice.

Dani grinned as she sat up, still stroking at the silvery white stuff on her leg, the echo of her fantasy last night. Mitch's semen had leapt as high into the air in reality as it had in her dream. Smoothing it slowly into her skin, she looked up at him, waiting for the inevitable comment.

As usual, Mitch didn't disappoint. 'It's supposed to be good for the skin,' he said blithely, struggling to his feet and then pulling up his underpants and shorts. 'I'd offer you some more, but even *I* can't supply it right this minute.' He squeezed his crotch by way of unsubtle emphasis.

Dani threw a handful of grass and mud at him.

'I appreciate the offer, but I'll stick with Oil of

'Okay, thanks. Now, do you think you could help me find my knickers?'

He did just that, and after a moment, he was helping her step into them.

Mitch might be Lothario and an unprincipled pervert, thought Dani as they began making their way back through the woods, but at least he's got decent manners with it. She'd felt quite pampered as he'd helped her with her clothes, and cherished in a way that was strangely sexless. For all his macho outrageousness, she was struck again by what a friend he'd become, and how much she felt able to trust him. Without an instant of worry or trepidation, she started telling him all about the fax.

'Any ideas who sent it?' she asked at length, 'I've made my own shortlist . . . but it all seems a little bit fanciful. It doesn't seem the sort of thing that a legitimate businessman . . . or woman . . . would do. It's too "cloak and dagger". Too Agatha Christie . . . We'll be finding a body in the library next.' She smiled as she thought of Cass – and her reference to another fictional detective.

Mitch seemed to consider this, and when Dani paused on the track and looked back at him, his face was enigmatic and thoughtful. They were almost out into the open now, and the sun was glancing off his glasses. It was impossible to see his eyes.

'There's no reason why an entrepreneur can't have a sense of humour,' he said after a while, his voice strangely neutral.

'But why send the fax to me?' she persisted, stung by his sudden detachment after what'd happened between them just minutes ago.

'Why not? You're the one who's on the desk most often. The one who does the *real* work around here ... You can't exactly call the management conscientious, can you?'

'Well, thanks for the reference, but I don't see how this MJK knows that . . .'

'Of course they know!' said Mitch, almost impatiently. 'We're being watched, aren't we?'

'I suppose so,' said Dani, perplexed. 'But I wish I knew who by . . . I hate this sort of thing. I have this overpowering urge to know things. I can't rest with any sort of mystery, I *have* to find out the answer. Not knowing just bugs me!'

Mitch grinned, caught up with her, and slung a casual but comforting arm around her. 'I'll tell you what, Miss Marple,' he said lightly, 'if you promise to be nice to me, and not threaten to kill me every time I fall from grace, I'll 'assist you with your enquiries'. Every great sleuth has a sidekick – and I'll be yours.' He winked, then slid his hand all the way down from her shoulder to the firm upper slope of her thigh. 'Just make sure you reward me in kind . . .'

'All right, but I'll thank you to keep your paws off for the moment,' said Dani, shaking free of him, and not sure whether she'd just gained an asset or a hindrance. 'I only pay out for results!'

7 The Ice Queen

LOIS FRENCH STARED intently at the fax log, and wondered where the missing entry was.

The machine had received *something* mid-morning, but there were no thin, flimsy sheets anywhere on the desk, and none in the in-tray either. The very emptiness made her feel nervous.

'Pull yourself together,' she chided under her breath, knowing it wasn't at all like her to panic. She prided herself on her sang-froid, but the changes that were looming at the Bouvier Manor had even given her the willies.

It was partially her fault, she supposed. Working at the hotel had brought her a fine sense of power, but also some lamentable lapses of judgement. Her natural desire for the good life, combined with Richard's susceptibility to her charms, had made her do things her keen mind knew were incautious. Things that had seemed so childishly easy; things she'd never in a million years have expected to be discovered. An amount enhanced here, a nought added there, the occasional fictional invoice. Such creative book-keeping had sunk without trace in the mire of a large hotel's accounting, the old owners being far too lazy and complacent to ever start looking for problems. The mysterious new owner *would* be looking however – probably with a shoal of barracuda auditors – and the discrepancies discovered and dealt with.

The idea of some kind of retribution made Lois's heart thud. The very word itself aroused her. Yes, she decided, licking her glossy red lips, someone would have to 'suffer' for this. She smiled to herself, feeling the stirrings of her fantasy persona. It wasn't her fault that trouble was looming, was it? She'd been let down, and Richard was partly to blame. If he'd shown a little more savoir-faire, this situation would never have arisen and her job and her status would have been safe.

Steepling her long polish-tipped fingers, Lois gave the matter some thought. Some deliciously escapist thought . . . She tried out a few of her favourite inner scenarios, her sure-fire tension-busters, and smiled again as she started feeling better. She consulted her mock Cartier watch, and saw that Daniella would be back on duty any time now. The girl could be left on Reception for as long as was necessary, and might even know something about the fax.

Ah, Daniella, thought Lois, feeling some of her rising arousal spill out towards the spirited young redhead. Daniella Stratton was as physically alluring as she was efficient, and in Lois's opinion, an irresistibly provocative challenge. It'd soon be time to make a move on the girl, to initiate her. Always providing that gypsy slut of a chambermaid hadn't got in there and done the deed first!

Not that Cass wasn't tempting herself. The Romany girl was rough trade by Lois's standards, but she had a steamy, knowing look about her that made the pulses race and the loins burn and quicken with lust. There'd be no gentle initiation required there, Lois decided. No coaxing, cajoling or deception. Dark, exotic Cass would know all the tricks – and then some.

Lois wondered if the gypsy was into discipline games already, then pictured that lush, tanned body in a skimpy French maid's costume: worn with silk stockings and not a single stitch of underwear. She'd be hot and ready, her vulva wet to the touch, and her pubic hair tangled and silky. Lois imagined tugging on it tantalisingly until Cass whimpered and bucked then taking her quickly and expertly with three fingers plunging stiffly in her channel and a thumb pressing down on her clitoris.

The fantasy was delightful, and as she sank even deeper into it, Lois suddenly realised how much it was affecting her. Without thinking, she was massaging her crotch against the corner of the hard office desk. Gasping with irritation, she stepped away and smoothed down her skirt. This was no time for casual diversions; she had to contain herself. And be ready for far, far more than just a hasty come against the edge of a desk.

Checking her immaculate appearance in the office mirror, Lois smoothed a non-existent wisp back into her chignon, then strode out into the main area of Reception, the image of businesslike efficiency. She was fully aware that the staff called her the 'Ice Queen', and she liked it, enjoying the concept of a chilly, unruffled power that had an inferno of heat at its heart.

Dani Stratton was just scampering down the main staircase, her auburn pony-tail swinging and her pretty cheeks looking somewhat flushed.

The staff weren't supposed to use the front stairs, but she'd obviously decided to risk it. Lois took a purely token look at her watch, then prepared to reprove the younger woman.

'Daniella,' she said, her voice unraised but still deadly, 'this isn't the time for the staff to be chasing up and down the main staircase, is it? And with things as they are, I'd prefer it if you'd remember to be punctual too.'

The expression on Dani's beautiful face was an amalgam of exasperation, defiance, and a half-hearted attempt to look sorry. Lois felt another hot rush of desire for the girl: a longing to see that bold spirit tempered, and that slender yet voluptuous body bearing up against physical correction.

Dani wouldn't grovel under pressure, thought Lois longingly. Dani would be resolute and feisty, and her bared flesh would be firm beneath the hand. Lois imagined the girl across her knee with her bottom uncovered and her stockings rolled halfway down her thighs. She imagined her staying very still under the strokes, then obediently dropping to the floor, crawling between Lois's thighs and extending a long, pink, and very flexible tongue—

'Sorry, Miss French,' said Dani quietly, her demeanour irreproachably demure. 'I went for a run in my break, and I forgot to put on my watch.'

Lois accepted the apology negligently, then began to outline the lunch-hour's developments. There were only routine matters really, but when these were covered, she raised the issue of the still missing fax.

'It was a wrong number!' the younger woman replied rather quickly. 'I pressed "receive" just in case it was somebody with an old machine or something.'

It was plausible, and Lois decided not to challenge Dani, but to save her suspicions for later. When maybe a little leverage would be useful?

On leaving Reception, Lois made her way up to her own apartment. She made a point of using the front staircase, and felt her usual delectable little frisson of one-upmanship as she left her subordinate behind her. When she reached the landing, she imagined that Dani had been watching her progress up the stairs, and admiring the sway of her bottom.

'I'll have you, you little darling,' she whispered as she reached the door to her small suite of rooms. The girl was wavering, and ripe for the taking . . .

Some time later, after a long, hot shower and a change of clothing, Lois felt full of a wild anticipation. Pouring herself a large gin and tonic from the supply she'd liberated from the cellar, she considered the interlude ahead of her.

Richard would be free this afternoon – as he was most afternoons – and right now he'd be waiting in his room, probably feeling all the same anticipation that she did. Their little after-lunch assignations had originally started out as a once a week thing, but had quickly increased to twice, or even three times or more.

Thus, almost every day, while Dani, or more recently, the rather tasty young Mitch was dutifully taking care of the guests and their queries, Lois was upstairs indulging herself. Enjoying her secret and favourite predilection with a man who was thrilled to indulge her.

Standing before her antique cheval glass, Lois sipped her drink, savouring its gut-kicking strength as she studied her own reflection. She'd let down her thick, straight, pale blonde hair so it hung in smooth sheaves to her shoulders. She'd re-applied her make-up, made it fierce and slightly stylised, then slid into clothing that matched it. A black silk fitted shirt worn without a bra, and a pair of Lycra jeans-cut trousers that clung ferociously to her contours like a coat of shimmering black paint. Beneath these she wore a G-string, a minuscule scrap of black French lace that was already thoroughly soaked with her juices. The hot, sleazy flow that the thought of a session with Richard had induced. Her final preparation was to slide her feet into short, soft boots; then, placing one or two choice items in her attaché case, she left her suite and made her way towards Richard's.

She didn't knock, because she knew he was waiting for her. Lying on his bed in just shirt and suit trousers, he had an icy drink on the chest of drawers beside him and a magazine open across his lap.

'I thought you'd be ready?' She kept her voice soft and silky, and her face neutral, knowing there was far more fun to be had by being subtle. Nevertheless, Richard rose from the bed immediately, his whole demeanour expressing his excitement as his magazine slid forgotten to the floor. With his sandy hair falling forward in his eyes, he was handsome in a smooth sort of way, but as he stood beside his bed, visibly trembling, his face was a picture of frustration and hunger. His stance was respectful, or at least appeared so, but his erection was huge, bulging and obscenely noticeable on a man who liked to play the role of submissive. Lois felt like walking up to him and squeezing him menacingly, but she knew how very much he'd love that, so decided to save it for later . . . as just one amongst a number of treats.

Richard's pale, well-kept fingers flew to his shirt buttons. Lois could see he was trying hard to get into his role, and keep his face meek and subservient, but he wasn't entirely succeeding. He was such a cocky beast in real life that she nearly cracked a grin – *and* broke the spell – when she saw him gnaw his lip theatrically in an expression that was supposed to be chagrin.

'Not that,' she said quietly, nodding that he should begin disrobing his lower body first.

Lois never shouted during encounters such as these. Crisp, controlled tones were far more effective, and her 'victims' were awed by her coolness. She sometimes felt a certain violence, but it always remained inside her, as fuel for an electrifying arousal. A degree of it was seething in her now, as she prowled slowly around the room, then placed her ominous case on the bed. Sexually, she felt like an overprimed bomb: her nipples were like stones, pulling tensely on the tissues of her breasts, and her vulva was drippingly uncomfortable. Very soon her seeping juices would darken the Lycra of her leggings, but if she caught Richard as much as glancing at her crotch, it'd be a good chance for another show of sternness.

Still buzzing from the drink in her room, Lois suddenly needed another. Richard had a cache of booze that had escaped the hotel's stocklist too, and as he began to fumble with his belt buckle, Lois prepared herself another stiff gin. There was something about the silvery resinous spirit that seemed to suit these occasions perfectly. Its flavour was steely and unyielding, and set fresh power flowing through her veins. She imagined dipping her finger in the glass and touching it to her clitoris, then hissing through her teeth at the spirit's angry bite. Turning away from Richard, she allowed herself a smile, wondering what he'd make of her hidden masochistic tendencies . . . Maybe next time they could try a different game.

'Still dressed?' she enquired, swinging around. Richard was only just unzipping his trousers, as if he were genuinely embarrassed to reveal the state of his penis.

Lois well knew what would be in his mind right now. Richard adored this moment of humiliation. Having to display his helplessly turned-on body to her was one of the early highlights of the show for him and he seemed to relish it all the more for being mocked.

As the smart grey tailoring slid down to his ankles, Lois gave a soft, contained laugh. Instead of boxer shorts Richard was wearing a pair of her own French knickers. Made of a shiny, burgundy silk, they would have looked ridiculous enough under normal circumstances, but now they were tented outwards at the front. The loose legs were gaping under the pressure of his erection, and a few twists of pubic hair were peeking out, plus just one of his swollen, reddish balls.

'Hmmm,' murmured Lois disparagingly. 'But what do we do with the shirt?'

This too was a regular ingredient of the game. Lois preferred Richard partly dressed for the first segment of the proceedings, and a feature of his debasement was that he held up the tails of his shirt himself, while Lois tugged down the borrowed knickers.

He obeyed quickly, clutching the bundled fabric above his belly button, then standing there waiting, the bulge in the ruby silk enormous. There was a spreading damp patch too, where his glans butted against the fabric, and Lois relished the evidence of his wetness. The tip of his cock was weeping uncontrollably, as if imitating a different and far sweeter kind of tears.

Slowly, at her leisure, she strolled forward, placed her drink beside his, then took hold of the waistband of the knickers. For a moment, she simply stretched the elastic slightly, looking directly into his lust-filled brown eyes, then with a measured, almost infinitesimal unhurriedness, she began easing the flimsy garment downwards.

This was a variation on the usual kind of dominance games. It wasn't usual for a mistress to perform such tasks, or to half-kneel before her awe-stricken plaything. But Lois enjoyed twists, and little changes to accepted procedures. She found they increased the state of high tension, and kept Richard delightfully off-balance. He gasped in surprise as she licked his shaft – just once – while she freed it, but when he flaunted his pelvis towards her, she leapt up and danced away, leaving her lingerie at half mast around his knees.

'Are you proud of that?' she enquired, reaching for her drink and taking a tiny sip. For a moment, she considered holding the gin in her mouth and kissing the crown of Richard's penis. The resulting protest would be highly amusing, but he'd also probably ejaculate, and Lois didn't want *that* just yet.

Richard didn't answer, but his face reddened.

'Well?' she persisted.

'I . . . I don't know,' he stammered, looking down at himself. Lois gave him a narrow-eyed 'what kind of an answer is that?' look and moved closer to inspect her property.

Richard's erection was so extreme now that it pointed straight upwards towards her, the flesh itself as solid as old oak.

I could hang something on that, she reflected whimsically, then ran through a few likely items. The knickers perhaps? She could make him step out of them, then drape them on his shaft himself . . .

What about her G-string? A good idea, but that would entail her stripping off too, something else that would make him come too soon. He'd spurt for sure if the fragrance of her sex touched his glans.

How silly you would look, thought Lois, feeling her blood stir and her mettle rise. She remembered this man from her interview, recalled his suave, self-important style, and how he'd almost preened like a peacock before her.

A representative of the Bouvier family had been there too, but he'd been an oldish man and easily impressed. Richard, on the other hand, had launched the interview with a fine show of ego-tripping and some obviously macho body language that would have worked on almost every other woman. Lois however had been piquantly amused, and because she'd already had several other good jobs offered to her that week, she'd decided to rise to his game and match it. Her own body language had been pure sex, but so unobtrusively executed that Richard had laid the job down before her within minutes, and been besotted before he was even aware of it. A condition he remained in to this day.

'Now, why not make it dance for me?', she said suddenly. 'Amuse me . . . You know how I get when I'm bored.'

With a red, red face, and with sweat breaking out along his hairline, Richard bent his knees slightly and began to rotate and jiggle his pelvis. His stiff flesh swayed to his rhythm, the fat head

86

bouncing and dipping in an action that was indeed faintly dance-like. Lois could well imagine that the effect on Richard was as stimulating as it was deeply shaming, the drag of air both caressing and tormenting.

'More,' she urged, then turned away and moistened her dry lips. Richard might get off on being a malleable toy for her, but he had a large, vigorous and easily hardened cock. Lois could feel her vagina fluttering furiously, as if it were demanding that she let him fill it. Soft, slippery fluid welled up in her and flowed out across her labia and clitoris, soaking the insubstantial lace of her G-string as she watched Richard's laughable contortions.

The temptation to rub herself was powerful, but resisting it was far more fun. The pit of her belly was like a pressure cooker; tight, out-swelling, and alive with unstoppable craving.

'It's not very impressive, is it?' she observed, dismissing the very flesh she longed to envelop. 'It looks as if it could be much much harder . . .' She cocked her head on one side, eyeing him, noting that he did in fact seem to be stiffening even as she watched, 'I think, perhaps, we should tickle it up a little . . . Don't you?'

'Oh no!' he whimpered, his brown eyes saying "yes yes yes!" 'Please, no!'

'Oh yes . . .' murmured Lois, the wild tension in her loins increasing. 'But first . . .'

This next part of the game was something Richard didn't like quite as much. But as Lois herself found it highly titillating, it was an element she often included.

Snapping open her attaché case, she drew out a pair of perfectly standard office bull-dog clips, then held them up so her companion could see them.

Keeping to his role, Richard whimpered and shook his head. Lois could see sweat rolling down his face now, and drops of it gathering on his lip. He was accustomed to the clips and their purpose, but at the same time half in love with them too.

'Dear God!' he cried as she tore open the few remaining buttons on his hand-made shirt, then deftly closed the clips on his nipples, one after the other.

'There . . . Isn't that pretty?' Lois asked as he licked the droplets of sweat from his lip, and momentarily she wished *she* could taste them. Down below, his penis was swelling, as if stretching out towards her, but teasingly she stepped back beyond his reach.

Richard's fingers tensed into fists. He was fighting inside now, trapped by the rules of their shadowplay. Lois knew that the small pain from the clips would be arousing him intensely – his cock told her so – yet to stay within his role he had to endure anything and everything without a murmur. Worst of all he had to fight his own pleasure.

Almost tasting his sensual dilemma, Lois gave Richard her most old-fashioned look. 'Continue,' she bade him, reaching for her drink and draining it. 'Touch yourself.'

Slowly, almost reluctantly, Richard complied.

As a female, Lois had no way of knowing exactly what it felt like when a penis was caressed, but she imagined that the sensations would be similar to those she experienced when she slicked her own swollen clitoris. Richard's flesh must be a bar of fire by now, aching for release just as her vulva ached to be stroked and fondled. He certainly *looked* profoundly uncomfortable, his shaft trembling, and coloured a violent, heavily veined crimson where it poked out between his nervously gripping fingers. It seemed to jut upwards at a steep, yearning angle, and his testicles were as dark as two plums.

'Shirt off now, Richard,' she said almost cajolingly, then paused to pour herself more gin. 'And you may step out of my underwear too . . .'

As she mixed her new drink, Lois silently commended her victim for having a large supply of ice. She was burning up in every way now, and the coolness of the gin was sublime. Flicking an ice cube with her tongue, she thought about the hotel's mischievous reputation. Was the water a turn-on? And if it was, what it would feel like to push a melting chunk of solid aphrodisiac right into the hot depths of her sex? Or maybe rub it against her clitoris? It was a load of superstitious nonsense, yet something was making her feel wicked. Or more accurately, wickeder. She looked down towards the now naked Richard, then glanced towards the contents of her case.

Taking time to plan her next refinement, Lois took another pull of gin, then signalled Richard towards a spot just in front of her.

Standing with legs parted and her hands resting lightly on hips, Lois felt the devil stir slyly in her belly. Her relationship with this man was at best very difficult to define. Sometimes she was irritated by him, sometimes she almost despised him, but at the heart of it all – unlikely as it seemed – there was a genuine core of affection. Richard might be a fool over a lot of things, but he understood her, especially her need for episodes like these. He might have very probably lost her a good job now, but his affinity with her strange desire for games was something that almost made her love him. Almost . . .

'Kneel on the bed,' she ordered coolly, 'Facing away from me, please . . .' she added, knowing that clinical politeness thrilled him far more than shows of mock-temper.

When he was in position, head bowed, she took a long silk scarf from her case and bound his hands at the small of his back. Eyeing a second scarf, she debated gagging him. She ran the slinky thing slowly through her fingers, loving its coolness, then thought about the sound of Richard's moans. With a smile, she dropped the scarf back in the case.

'Forward now,' she said, pushing firmly on the nape of his neck. 'Press your forehead against the cover, but don't let your penis touch the bed.' She let her hand drop delicately on to his bottom. 'Or you'll be sorry,' she added with a delicate but significant firmness.

Richard's rump was really his best feature, thought Lois dispassionately, admiring the hard muscle, the masculine dimples, and the narrow, shadowy groove. She smiled when she saw his thighs flex and his anus pout, as if inviting her. I wouldn't encourage me, if I were you, she told him silently, reaching carefully into the depths of her case.

'Relax,' she whispered, hefting the slender black object she'd selected. Swivelling the bevelled knob on one end of it, she nodded approvingly when it set up a soft, even hum. 'Relax,' she whispered again, then before Richard could protest, or even comprehend what she was doing, she passed the vibrator across the cheeks of his bottom, then let it rest for a second between them.

Almost instantly, he started squirming, and begging vociferously that she stop what she was doing, although every line of his body begged for more.

Oh yes! thought Lois exultantly, entranced by the waggling of his bottom. 'Stay still!' she ordered, repeating the action of before but more tantalisingly, letting the vibrator dawdle against his trembling perineum.

After a minute or two, he was a gasping, panting wreck, his chest heaving and his bottom cheeks taut and clenching. Each time he seemed about to lose control, Lois paused, and fondled him with her fingers only, touching his balls or his tight anal ring.

'Please . . . Oh God,' he pleaded as she teased him again. He was obviously in two minds about what he wanted, and beside himself with sensation, but Lois chose to believe – from the way his whole body jiggled and jerked – that it was still *more* that he wanted, not less.

Slowly and tauntingly, she ran the vibrator all over his hind parts: tickling the tiny hole with it, flicking at his inner thighs, and floating the tip of it very gently over his balls.

Richard was moaning uninhibitedly now, pushing his face into the counterpane and gasping. His thighs were rigid with effort, his belly taut, and his cock diamond-hard. Lois had never seen such a vision of blissful submission in her life, and neither had she ever felt as randy. As she shifted her position on the bed, the seam of her jeans grazed her clitoris. Her gleaming black sex toy slipped nervelessly from her fingers and she orgasmed immediately, stifling her hoarse cry of pleasure with her fist. In total silence, she climaxed long and hard, but revealed not a trace of it to Richard.

The spasms took some time to subside, and to

calm herself she watched the slow, pulsing twitch of Richard's bottom. The strain of not coming must be killing him, she thought, feeling soft and decidedly mellow as her own flesh glowed with satisfaction. His penis was as unbending as a cast iron rod, and his pre-ejaculatory nectar shone clearly on its jutting head.

Orgasm had purged Lois of many of her negative feelings. She still blamed Richard for putting both their futures at risk, but her over-riding emotion was a magnanimous, almost affectionate indulgence. Let the little boy have his fun now, Lois, she told herself, feeling loose and sensuously genial, queenlike but no longer quite so icy . . .

'Right, that's it, my sweet, it's time to do the thing you like best,' she said, touching him cautiously on his agitated flank then making short work of his thin, silky bonds.

When he was free, Richard slumped on his side, breathing heavily, but quite still, as if waiting as patiently as he could for his treat. Coming up over him, Lois stroked his quivering haunches, then slowly, oh so carefully, and with a lot of encouragement and soothing, slid the smooth tip of the vibrator inside him and stretched his sphincter with its softly purring girth. When it was lodged half in and half out of him, she reached down, took his hand, and folded it snugly around his cock.

Richard's sweaty face was a picture of ecstasy, and in seconds, with few jerky strokes, he was coming, his pearly semen shooting out in jets that flew halfway across the rumpled bed. As he came, he muttered garbled words of pleasure and thanks, but seemed unable to open his eyes. When it was finally over, and his penis was shrinking and sticky, he curled up into a loose foetal shape, as if the experience had robbed him of his strength. Looking down, Lois blew him a kiss . . .

It was her turn to wait now, and as she too lay on the bed, Lois let her consciousness drift. Her attention flitted aimlessly from image to image and eventually settled on a favourite. The superb female form of Dani Stratton.

The girl was lush and pretty and intelligent. Far *too* intelligent really. Lois felt a pang of disquiet as she pictured those over-bright eyes so full of sharp, incisive savvy. It wouldn't be a surprise if Dani knew all about the hotel's financial 'irregularities' and was biding her time – until she could use her secret knowledge to some advantage.

Lois quivered. It was that thin, sweet edge of danger that made Dani Stratton so wantable, and not for the first time, Lois spooled out one of her choicest scenarios. She'd caught Dani alone in a secluded hidey-hole: the wine-cellar, the linen cupboard, or perhaps the dim, cool vegetable store, outside in the old kitchen yard. She imagined herself opening the door to the shed, and finding Dani inside, crouched amongst the sacks, masturbating. Her slim, tight skirt would be rucked around her waist, and her white panties pooled around her ankles. Lois could almost smell the girl's juices, and see them, thick, clear and glistening, as she looked down at that dainty, russet-haired cleft.

She'd knock Dani's hand away, and replace it with her own, coating a fingertip with the copious dew and transferring it to the girl's throbbing clitoris . . .

Dani would cry out, and her hips would jump.

93

Her beautiful, fine-featured face would crumple in a paroxysm of pleasure, and more fluid would gush out on to Lois's hand.

And as her victim arced and bucked, burbling words of praise and adoration, Lois too would fall down amongst the potatoes and the turnips, and press her crotch against Dani's stockinged thigh . . .

A sigh put a stop to the fantasy. Lois took her hand from her crotch – where it had naturally settled – and looked up towards the source of the interruption.

Richard was a sorry but contented-looking sight. His hair was wet with perspiration, his body blanched and shaky, and his penis a tiny, shrunken stub. Why did men often look so pathetic in the aftermath? Lois wondered wryly. Even the smooth bastards like Richard. A woman in the same situation usually had far more composure. Dani would, in particular . . . and also that swarthy minx Cass.

'Come here,' said Lois lazily. Spreading her legs, she hitched her bottom forward to the edge of the bed and set her feet flat on the carpet. 'You know what to do.'

Richard slid off the bed, then hovered a foot away from her knees. Closing her eyes, she let herself go limp and let him fumble first with her boots, and then with her skin-tight trousers. As her mind flew high and free, other hands – not Richard's – went to work on her tiny, sopping G-string.

'Come on . . . Get a move on,' she said, feeling impatient with him now she was exposed. 'Make yourself useful . . .'

A tongue settled clumsily on her clitoris, but lost in fantasies, she'd already forgotten whose.

In her dreams, a female mouth sucked her. First Dani's, then Cass's, then other less familiar women. Hotel guests, acquaintances, film stars, women she'd seen just once, on the street or in shops. Curling her toes, she wondered if that hoity-toity authoress in Suite 17 liked licking pussy, then imagined Pandora Barrie crouched worshipfully between her legs, her pointy face wet and smeared with juice.

When the tongue became bolder, and more sure of itself, the kneeling figure transposed itself again. This time the licking supplicant was Mrs Amy Lovingood – the confident, impressive 'woman of a certain age' to whom Lois had been instantly attracted. A woman who could do exactly what she wanted and take any young lover she pleased . . .

And then it was Dani again, then Cass, then both of them, huddled between her legs, lapping, suckling and mouthing, and using their fingers with precision and daring.

Reality slid away into the void as a digit bored rudely into her bottom, and another smoothly entered her sex. Hard teeth nipped cruelly at her tiny bud of pleasure; then more softly, lips playfully worried it, and rolled it to and fro and back and forth.

Growling and thrashing, Lois saw colours rainbow bright behind her eyelids and heard distorted sounds pounding in the distance. Orgasm grabbed her loins like a fist, and one noise surfaced above all others – a steadily rapping beat that seemed to synchronise with the pulsing of her clitoris.

'Yes! Yes! Yes!' she screamed as the sensations meshed, and her whole sex danced with leaping fire.

In the numbed aftermath, as her body returned slowly to normal, Lois felt a strange new awareness. In her dazed mind, the last few moments replayed themselves, but not from her inner perspective. Detachedly, analytically, she heard again an insistent knock at the door, then faintly a voice calling, and finally, the door itself opening.

Almost afraid of what she might see, Lois opened her leaden eyelids, and saw – beyond the still kneeling Richard – a figure both challenging and familiar . . .

Her eyes wide and almost black with fascination, Cassandra Jenkins was standing just three yards away, with the laundry stock book open in her hand. As Lois watched, it dropped, forgotten, to the floor, and the gypsy licked her full, red lips.

'Is this a private party, or can anyone play?' enquired Cass, then stepped forward, her fingers working quickly on her buttons.

8   Girl Talk

'*SO WHAT DID* you do then?'

Dani could hardly believe what she was hearing, but as Cass had sworn that everything was true, there was no doubt it genuinely was.

'Well . . . What else could I do? I just stripped off, shoved Richard out of the way, and took over where he'd left off.' The Romany girl paused and took a drink of the wine Dani had just poured. 'He really is useless, you know, he just crawled into a corner, curled up and watched us. Pathetic! If it'd been Mitch, he'd have joined in the fun . . .'

Dani took a long pull from her own glass, then reached for the bottle and topped up again. It was bedtime, and Cass had come around to her room for a chat, as she often did, but tonight their casual girl-talk was like nothing Dani had ever heard before.

She'd known for some time that Cass was a sexual switch-hitter. The signs had always been there – some subtle, some less so – but this was the first time the gypsy girl had spoken overtly of being lesbian. Dani knew she shouldn't be shocked, but somehow she was. It was her own feelings that were causing all the trouble though, her confusion and her jealous desire. Her brain was flooded with bright images, and in them it was Cass kissing *her*.

'You're a lesbian, aren't you?' she demanded suddenly, amazed at the shrewish harshness of her voice in the small, cosy confines of her room.

'Well, glory be, I thought you'd never catch on!' Cass's dark eyes twinkled. 'Considering that you're the cleverest person I've ever met, Dani Stratton, it's taken you one helluva long time to see the obvious!'

'I . . . I thought it might be a secret.'

Cass threw back her head and laughed out loud, her white teeth flashing in the lamplight, and her mouth a tempting gash of rosy red.

'I don't give a monkey's who knows,' she said cheerfully, then suddenly her captivating face turned solemn. 'Just as long as *you* don't mind.'

'No . . . I . . . It makes no difference to me,' answered Dani, not sure whether it did or not.

'To be strictly correct, sweetheart,' Cass went on, stretching languidly on Dani's narrow bed, 'I'm bisexual, not lesbian. It's the best of both worlds. When there aren't any cute men available, I can always make whoopee with a girl.'

Dani absorbed the statement, and detected her friend's slight emphasis, but still felt the shackles of anxiety. Cass was beautiful, and eminently lovable, but trepidation and nerves held Dani back. She couldn't imagine Cass's touch being anything less than delectable, but wanting her – wanting her mouth, her fingers, and her sex – was like taking the giantest of adrenaline-filled leaps.

Nevertheless, she was curious. 'So . . . Tell me about making whoopee with the "Ice Queen" then,' she asked, sipping her cool, golden wine to keep calm.

'Mmmmm . . . She's not cool at all when you get up close,' murmured Cass dreamily, shifting her ripe body slightly on the bedspread. Her nipples were two vivid blurs beneath her white cotton robe, like dark berries wrapped in wafer-thin tissue. Dani had a sudden, quite alarming urge to bite them.

As Cass spoke of her strange encounter with the hotel's Assistant Manager, her voice was animated yet peculiarly matter-of-fact. Dani supposed it was all perfectly normal to her friend. That stripping another woman naked and tasting every inch of her body was something quite familiar and acceptable. As was pushing your fingers into her sex and her anus, and mouthing her breasts and letting her mouth yours . . .

Drinking steadily, Dani listened with increasing attention to Cass's description of her antics. How she'd straddled Lois's cool, perfect face and ridden her slowly lapping tongue. The account was vivid, almost electric, and punctuated with sighs of real, remembered pleasure. Dani couldn't help but imagine herself in her gypsy friend's place.

But the substitution was muddled. As she put aside her glass and lay back amongst the pillows, head to tail with Cass, it was Cass in her mind doing the licking. It was Cass's long, cherry-pink tongue travelling slowly over her fire-hot membranes and cooling them with gentleness and spittle. Cass sucking, Cass touching, Cass's slender, ingenious fingers feathering at places both sensitive and forbidden.

Wracked with confusion, Dani opened her mouth to ask a barely-formed question, then closed it again, and just listened. Intensely and unbearably aroused, she was paralysed by her friend's smoky voice.

99

'She wasn't wearing a bra,' breathed Cass, 'just that black silk shirt and nothing else. I wanted to pinch her nipples till she squealed . . . To pay her back for being such a bitch. But when I actually did it, she just went mental. Squirming all over the place, begging for "more!" and shoving my hand into her crotch. I thought I was a horny beggar, but Lois is insatiable. I've no idea what'd happened before I arrived, but she had at least four orgasms on *my* tongue and she was still screaming for it! Can you believe that?'

Dani could, and bit her lip against her own cries of need. Maybe it was the wine – or perhaps the Bouvier Manor water – but suddenly the great leap had been accomplished. At some unnoticed instant in the last few minutes, her sexuality had been profoundly re-configured. She looked at Cass, and saw tawny skin that she wanted to kiss, tumbling, ethnicised black curls that she wanted to rub against her breasts and her belly, and an opulent, scarcely clad body that she wanted to massage with the whole length of her own. The woman before her was a poem of pleasure: firm flesh, nimble fingers, and a tongue that was long, sleek and wet . . .

'Cassie?' she whispered, still unsure how to ask for what she wanted.

Cass gazed back from the other end of the bed. Her strange, slanted eyes were sloe-dark in the half-light, and glowing with a fund of ancient wisdom. She knew, it was clear. Knew exactly what Dani wanted and needed. Rising like a nymph from her resting place, she seemed to flow over the narrow space between them, and lose her thin cotton wrap in the process. Crouching over Dani's trembling body, she was transformed from a nymph into a goddess, a naked and

100

bountiful deity intent on bestowing a sweet gift.

'Baby,' she whispered, making short work of Dani's pyjama buttons. 'Baby,' she breathed again, her mouth fastening softly on Dani's and prising it open very tenderly as her fingers began circling on her breasts.

It was a strong kiss, forceful yet circumspect, in the manner of dominant male lover. As her mouth was pillaged, Dani could almost imagine it was Mitch about to climb over her. Mitch arranging his body full length on top of hers, chest to chest and nipple to nipple.

But Mitch didn't have lush, pillow-soft breasts to press against her, and he didn't smell of lavender and femininity. Neither was his hair a tangle of trailing, fluffy-soft dreadlocks that were a delightful caress in themselves as they tickled and floated across her skin. Mitch was hard and male, and Cass was pliant and female, but faced with the two of them, Dani knew a choice would be almost impossible.

But it was Cass who was here, now, and kissing her.

'I've been dying for this,' whispered the gypsy, her mouth against Dani's trembling throat, 'All these months . . . It's been driving me insane. Wanting to touch you. Wanting to kiss you. Seeing you in your robe, and in your leotard, and in your swimsuit . . . Wanting to see you naked and spread open just for me.'

Soft fingers cupped Dani's right breast, weighing the flesh and testing its resilience. 'Oh God, you're so luscious,' purred Cass, squeezing firmly, then flicking at the crest with the tip of her finger and setting Dani's body wriggling in response.

The fondling of her breasts wasn't new to Dani;

men loved her full, curvy body, and often spent long hours exploring it. The novelty was in the slenderness of the hand that held her, and the finesse and pure accuracy of the touch. No man could know so well what was perfect and pleasurable, because no man had breasts of his own.

Just as she was about to moan for more, Dani felt Cass's weight shift, and saw her dark head start working slowly downwards. In an instant she was sucking Dani's nipple, drawing it hungrily and wetly into her mouth, and tugging like a baby taking milk.

The sensation was puzzling and beautiful, and reached deep into Dani's churning vitals. She looked down at her sweet gypsy lover, and felt an exquisite and melting affection. Cass was wild and divine and kindly; she'd wanted this all along, but held back out of consideration for an untutored friend. Almost weeping with confusion and gratitude, Dani rubbed her fingers over Cass's gilded back and relished its warmth, and its silky, vital smoothness.

'Be naked for me, darling,' purred Cass, rising up over her, her eyes dark and smudgy with passion. 'Your body is so perfect, Dani-love, I want to see all of it. I want to kiss your ribs and your belly button. I want to taste the insides of your knees. I want to touch your soft, sweet pussy and bury the whole of my hand in it. I want to make love to every single bit of you, and make you come until you can't come any more!'

Giggling and kissing, they achieved their objective in moments. Cass growled like a she-cat as Dani's pyjama bottoms slid off over her feet. Snatching up the thin, satin garment, she sent it flying through the air in high triumph, then plunged her hand between her friend's parted legs.

Dani cried out fiercely as a tip of a strong, clean, well-scrubbed finger took possession of her hungering clitoris. Her cries turned to crazed, frantic yelps as the fingertip manipulated her tiny, jumping bud with precisely the degree of force that she needed, nudging it from side to side and up and down, then jabbing like a marksman at its apex. No man had ever rubbed her quite like this.

Through a haze of jumbled impressions, Dani looked up adoringly at her new female lover.

The gypsy girl was kneeling on the bed now, her thigh next to Dani's, and her expression endearingly intent. She was concentrating totally on the movements of her fingers, and studying the wet, pink field of operations like a general mapping brand new terrain. Each daring foray was matched by a flicker of emotion on her lovely sun-kissed face. Frowning, she sucked lavishly on her finger, coated it shiny with spittle, then pushed it slowly into Dani's waiting body.

Dani felt speared, both by feeling and by flesh. It seemed as if Cass's spirit was inside her too, and that some arcane and sensual magic had been carried in on the unrelenting digit to reside at her hot and throbbing core. A new wave of concentric, flowing ripples began and her inner muscles grabbed hard at the intruder. She heard her voice soar skywards in a scream, and seemed to see it hover like a bubble in the air. Her hands scrabbled, grasping at any part of Cass she could reach, and then she was panting with ecstasy and thankfulness as the other woman bent down and kissed her lips.

There was a crude name for what Cass was

doing to her, Dani realised. Something hard and very masculine which in no way expressed such a gracious and feminine possession. Cass's mouth was alive with a primal, sucking power, and her finger seemed to plunge in far deeper than any mere cock had ever managed.

Dani felt tyrannised; taken; ploughed. She felt weak, yet incredibly strong and happy, transformed by the marvellous and the new.

After a moment, or perhaps a lifetime, Cass lay down beside her, pressing her body against the sweat on Dani's flanks while her finger stayed still in its niche.

'So . . . ' she whispered, her voice rich and seductive, 'what does it feel like to be fucked by a woman?'

It was the word that Dani had thought of, yet on Cass's sultry lips it was bewitching, a symbol of raw, unfiltered power.

'That's what it is, baby,' persisted Cass, jerking her finger. 'When I do this!' Again, and deeper . . . 'I'm fucking you, do you understand?'

Dani nodded, started writhing, and came again on the thing inside her sex. As she spasmed, she felt Cass working her deliberately, as if the other woman sensed in her a profound need for roughness that Dani herself had barely been aware of. Women-to-woman lovemaking had all the vigour and dynamism, she thought exultantly, of anything she'd ever experienced with men. All the spontaneity; all the downright down-and-dirty balls. She almost laughed at that, but the laugh changed suddenly to a shriek . . . as yet another wrenching climax raced through her.

It was kisses that eventually brought Dani to her senses. Small, shy, nibbling little kisses on her face, her throat and her jaw. Moving her legs, she became aware that her vagina was her own again, yet perversely she missed the rude, probing finger that had been in her for what seemed like hours and hours. With her eyes still closed, she reached out, searching blindly for the beloved warmth of Cass.

'Greedy baby,' cooed Cass from nearby. 'Do you want some more?'

'Yes! No! I don't know . . . ' Dani answered, not sure what she wanted, but guilty at the same time, because whatever it was, Cass hadn't had any of it yet.

'I should do something for you now, Cassie, shouldn't I?' she said uncertainly, opening her eyes.

Cass was sitting naked at the end of the bed, a full glass of wine in her hand. She looked calm and perfectly content; if she was sexually frustrated, it certainly didn't show.

'You don't have to, you know,' replied Cass softly, setting aside her glass. 'It isn't the same as it is with men . . . There's no "owing" each other anything. No rights. No "trade-offs". Woman-love's a tad more generous.'

'But don't you want an orgasm?' Dani asked, sitting up. As she reached for her own glass, now re-filled, she was acutely aware of Cass watching her proud, swaying breasts. What the gypsy said, and what she felt, could well be two quite different things.

'Yes, I do,' Cass replied frankly, 'very much so . . . But not this very instant. I feel turned-on . . . but I enjoy "wanting" as much as I do "getting".' She paused thoughtfully. 'I've always been so used to travelling in my life that sometimes I don't *need* to arrive.'

'A philosopher, eh?' observed Dani, beginning

to feel much more settled. Cass was still her friend, it seemed. Still as comfortable and easy to be with, even though now she was a lover as well.

'Of sorts,' the other girl murmured, looking shy herself all of a sudden, 'Look, Dani, I . . . I meant to be more gentle, you know . . . Work up to it gradually.' She put down her glass and licked her ruby-tinted lips, adding a gloss to their natural healthy glow. 'But I'd been waiting so long. Dreaming of this . . . ' She made a slight, graceful gesture that could've been anything, but to Dani spoke patently of sex.

'I shouldn't have made you wait,' Dani said evenly, 'It's been in my mind too, but I've been acting a bit dense these past few weeks. Ignoring the obvious . . . ' She reached out, moved forward, took Cass's long, warm hand. 'The obvious in me, Cass, as well as in you.'

Cass just smiled, inclining her luscious form temptingly towards Dani, her big slanted eyes dark and slumberous.

Dani felt her fears rush back. She wanted Cass again, and this time understood her own feelings, but what she didn't know was how to get things started. Cass had done it effortlessly because she was used to seducing other women. Dani had no other experience but now . . .

What would I want? she pondered, putting her fingers out haltingly towards Cass. What *do* I want? She looked at Cass's tender mouth, imagined it settling on her sex . . . and suddenly knew *exactly* what to do.

Drawing her friend close, Dani started kissing Cass's shoulder. The skin she encountered was smooth and very fine, slightly salty where it lay beneath her tongue. Cass was excited and perspiring freely, and Dani could taste its mineral residue on her skin. Running her hands up and down Cass's hips and waist, she extended the area of her kissing, planting her tiny, exploratory pecks on the upper slopes of the other woman's breasts. Cass's hands were moving now too, stroking Dani's neck and the luxuriance of her hair.

'Yes, love, yes,' whispered Cass, already shifting her hips from side to side in a frenzy, 'That's it,' she encouraged, 'Kiss me! I love it! Kiss me everywhere!'

Cass's nipples were as large and firm as two corks, and taking one in her mouth, Dani pursed her lips and used them to massage it.

Cass wailed as if she'd been bitten, the noise enormous in the small, cluttered room. Dani pulled back quickly, wondering if the pressure she'd exerted was too great.

'No! Please! Don't stop!' begged Cass, lacing her fingers behind Dani's head and pulling her down again, 'My breasts . . . Oh God, yes! I have orgasms just from . . . Oooooh! Oh Dani!' As Dani resumed her sucking Cass faltered, her writhings even wilder than before.

Stroking one of Cass's breasts and using her mouth on the other, Dani understood an aching truth. 'Giving' *was* as extraordinary as 'receiving', and Cass's nipple in her mouth turned her on. Her vulva quivered with pleasure as she sucked her friend's breast, even though there was no hand free to touch it or caress it.

Beneath her, Cass's response seemed out of all proportion. She was moaning and cooing, and waving her pelvis in a strange manic rhythm. Dani could almost believe her friend really was climaxing already; and if she wasn't, Dani was determined she would be soon.

107

Leaving Cass's nipples wet and swollen, she began to work her way downwards, kissing Cass's beautiful and softly rounded belly. The skin there was even finer, and especially delicate in the creases of her groin. Playing at first one side, then the other, Dani suddenly found that teasing was easy. Promising fulfilment, she took her mouth to within an inch of Cass's sanctum, then pulled back again and kissed her chastely on the hip.

'You bitch! You little bitch!' Cass's voice was full of laughter and frustration. 'Why don't you do it? Why don't you kiss me? You know I'm going crazy for your tongue!'

'Open your legs,' said Dani softly, easing her body into the optimum position. She was in unknown territory now ... She'd kissed cocks often enough, and enjoyed the process immensely, but the geography of a woman was quite different. Less obvious, but more elegant and subtle ...

'You've got to help me, Cassie,' she said firmly, 'It's all new ... I mightn't do it right. You've got to tell me what's right and what's wrong.'

'Don't worry, I will!' cried Cass, her voice almost gravelling with feeling. 'Just get on with it, you minx, I'm dying!'

'Open up,' Dani urged again, her palms on Cass's silky thighs. She needed light; she needed to see; and she needed as much space as possible for her manoeuvres so she could give her friend all the joy she deserved.

With a broken groan, Cass complied, forcing her tanned legs almost obscenely wide open.

Dani could see plum-dark love-lips pouting, and around them, a thick, glossy bush of jet-black hair. She could see a hundred different shades of magenta, a large and very prominent clitoris, and the tight vaginal portal farther back. She could actually see her friend's most intimate membranes moving, the flickering beckoning lewdly to her tongue. She could see living proof of Cass's raging, white-hot lust, and with a happy smile she leant forward to make it hers.

The perfume of Cass's vulva was rich and spicy, heavy with musk yet in another way exquisitely fresh. It rose up from between her legs like an irresistible magic potion, and when Dani tasted it, she wasn't disappointed.

Cass tasted just how she smelt, but if anything, a hundred times more delicious. Dani's mouth filled with saliva, and almost rabidly, she began to lick and lap – an instant addict to the charms of female flesh.

And it wasn't just the taste. The very convolutions of Cass's sex were enchanting. Her mouth continuing to water, Dani first examined the leaf-like folds of Cassie's inner labia, and savoured their spongy, swollen texture. The little lips were fat with blood, and protruding, their surface like silk with flowing juices. Making a small sound of appreciation, Dani sucked each one in turn into her mouth, tugged very gently, then laughed when Cass moaned and protested.

'I know ... I know ...' Dani murmured, because she *did* know what Cass was really wanting. Her own sex was screaming for the same.

Her clitoris felt as hot as fire, and seemed to stand out from her body like a stud. She wanted someone to pinch it, bite it, or pull on it. Jerk it roughly, and punish it till she came. No genteel feathery caress would satisfy her now, and she knew it wouldn't do for Cass either. With a low shaking growl of sexual fury, she pressed her face between her friend's flailing legs, took her clitoris tight between her lips, and sucked on it long, long and hard.

Cass shrieked, and her nails gouged Dani's shoulders like talons. Still sucking diligently, Dani felt the whole of her friend's pussy almost beating against her face like a tom-tom, and as she reached down between her own thighs, it took just one touch to bring herself to pleasure too.

'Like a duck to water,' observed Cass smugly, making the appropriate action amongst the bubbles of her bath. Dani blushed and got on with drying her hair.

After so much sweaty, satisfying sex, the two of them had decided to take a bath. Dani's tiny room had been thick with musky, female odours, so they'd opened the window, grabbed some towels, and padded naked and giggling down the corridor.

'You're right, of course,' answered Dani. 'It did come naturally . . . Once I got started. I must've been a lesbian all along.'

'Bisexual,' corrected Cass, soaping her breasts for what seemed the dozenth time. Dani smiled fondly, thinking of her friend's almost pathological obsession with cleanliness.

When Cass had been a traveller, baths or even washes had been difficult to come by, and personal hygiene a constant, hard-fought battle. But now that she had settled in one place for a while, she was in the bath at the slightest opportunity, and loved to wallow in a steaming tub for hours. Dani had an ominous feeling that this habit was going to get her friend in a different kind of hot water before long – because Cass had been known to try the guest bathrooms too!

'You're bisexual, Dani,' Cass reiterated cheerfully. 'You do still like men, don't you? I'm sure I certainly do!'

'Oh, I still like men all right,' Dani said dreamily, reaching for a wide-toothed comb to de-tangle her hair. Even as she'd spoken, she'd suddenly seen the image of Mitch again – half-naked, in a shady forest glade.

'And just who is that sleazy look in aid of?' Cass's dark eyes obviously missed nothing. 'Could it be young Mitchell, I wonder?'

'Why do you say that?' said Dani warily, her heart beating fast. Had they given themselves away somehow? Cass was a notorious 'observer' . . . Had she seen them in the woods? Or worse still, had Mitch himself been boasting? Dani knew she'd die of embarrassment if he'd told Cass what had happened beneath the desk . . .

'Don't panic!' said Cass gently. 'It's just the way he looks at you . . . I was watching, the other day, when you were showing some big-wig up to his room, and Mitch was carrying luggage just behind you. He was staring at your bottom as if his life depended on it, and he had a hard-on the size of a house!'

The news was nothing new, but curiously Dani felt elated. It proved that Mitch wasn't just teasing her, that he was as much out of control as she was. She smiled, feeling much more kindly disposed towards him, although she still thought his tricks were demonic.

Then another thought occurred. 'Cass . . .' she said cautiously, at a loss how to frame it.

'Okay, I admit it,' said Cass, pre-empting her.

'Admit what?'

'That I've had Mitch.'

111

Dani couldn't find it in her to be angry, and when she thought about it, she didn't really have the right to be. Mitch could be said to have 'betrayed her' with Cass, but hadn't she just done the same to him? *Also* with Cass . . . And weren't they all completely free agents anyway?

'So . . . Come on . . . Tell me everything,' she said, feeling a frisson of titillating naughtiness. Suddenly she wanted to hear all the juicy bits . . .

'It was a couple of days after he started,' began Cass, squeezing the loofah over the swell of her breasts. 'Do you remember all that hoo-hah about the laundry bills, when we had to check the sheets and stuff?'

Dani nodded. It was yet another of Lois and Richard's fiddles that she was trying her best not to fret about.

'Well, Mitch and I were in the big laundry cupboard and it just sort of happened.'

'Cass!' said Dani, mock-reproving.

'He was quizzing me about the hotel and how it was run and stuff . . . and somehow we got on to the subject of the water and whether it really made you horny. He asked me if it was true, and I said it was useless asking me because I feel horny all the time! Especially when there are cute young men with biteable bottoms about—'

'Oh God, Cass, you didn't say that, did you?' Dani was giggling as she spoke, knowing full well that Cass probably really *had* said it.

'More or less . . .'

'What next?'

'He said he thought my bottom was pretty biteable too . . . and one thing sort of led to another.'

Dani could imagine the scene. And imagine how Cass and Mitch must have found each other

112

fatally tempting. Faintly jealous, but not quite sure who of, she pictured her two friends embracing. Then kissing. Then naked, their bodies joined and pumping in a furious, energetic bout of sex.

When she looked across at the real Cass of here and now, Dani saw that the gypsy girl's eyes were dark and hazy. She was deeper in the water now too, and the froth on the surface was rocking. Both Cass's hands were hidden.

'I asked him if he wanted to see it . . . See my bottom, that is. And he nodded.' As if she'd quite forgotten Dani altogether, Cass let out a long, broken gasp. It was perfectly clear that beneath the foam she was masturbating. Giving pleasure to her vital, sexy body while her wild, inventive mind turned her on.

'So I leant over one of the big laundry baskets and pulled up my skirt.'

'I don't suppose you had any panties on, did you?' Dani knew for a fact that Cass usually scorned underwear completely, but somehow the question was exciting. As was the image her friend's bare rump beneath her smock, something she realised now that she'd thought of fairly often. Thought of, and speculated on; wondering what would happen if she crept up behind Cass while she was dusting or polishing, and slid a searching hand right up her skirt.

'I didn't look round. I didn't do anything,' Cass continued, her voice faint and breathy. 'I could feel him coming towards me, and I just lay there – offering him my backside and my sex.' She faltered, whimpered, and water sloshed over the side of the bath, 'I didn't give a damn what he did to me, as long as he did something . . . He could've had my pussy, or my arse or even both!'

113

Aroused again, Dani could feel her own nectar flowing; her own sex swelling as Cassie's had – both then and in the reality of now.

'He didn't touch me, caress me, or kiss me . . . I just heard a zip, then felt this huge, gorgeous thing pushing into me . . . So big, so hot. Stretching me . . . Really really stretching me . . .'

'Wh . . . where?' stammered Dani, shocked rigid that she should *want* it to be buggery.

'My pussy . . . First . . . Ungh . . . ungh . . . Oh God!' The water surged like a whirlpool, and for a moment Cass almost went under. She was thrashing and twisting – and obviously coming – and as her thick hair tumbled down all around her, the fluffy black locks were getting soaked.

Dani thought Cass looked like a mermaid, a beautiful, otherworldly sex-sprite, and the sight made her own sex judder.

Desperately turned on again, she dropped her comb and reached unashamedly downwards, rubbing her pussy just as Cass was rubbing hers.

Her climax came in an instant. Great, climbing waves of sensation lashed through her as her thoughts lost cohesion and form . . .

Was it Cass she was coming for – or Mitch? There was no way on earth she could tell. There was nothing to do but give in to it and just surrender to the pleasure itself.

9 Suspicions

THE NEXT MORNING, Dani woke up not knowing whether to be excited or worried. Life at the Bouvier Manor was so complicated now, so fraught with lust and sexuality that it almost seemed as if the 'water' tales were true.

To date, she was 'involved' with both Cass *and* Mitch, and if Cass's wild claims were to be believed, there was every likelihood *Lois* was interested too.

All it needed now was for Richard to come on to her, and the guests to get fresh, and she'd more or less got a full house!

Funnily enough though, as the morning wore on, Dani began to relish the pervading eroticism. She found herself flirting outrageously with Jamie Rivera, and making a special point of smiling and joking with him whenever Mitch passed through Reception on an errand.

In her heart of hearts, she didn't see her nemesis as a jealous type, but his insolent, 'couldn't care less' grins and the laughing glint in his bespectacled eyes were infuriating. He really didn't seem bothered whether other men hung around her or not, and her pride was thoroughly piqued. In consequence, she paid even more attention to Jamie Rivera. So much so that the famous tennis player almost seemed to be under her spell. He was still at the desk, chatting, when Mitch passed by the desk for the fourth or fifth time that morning.

The reaction this time was an unashamedly salacious wink, and without thinking Dani gave him her most narrow-eyed 'please die' look.

'Is that guy bothering you?' enquired Jamie Rivera in his distinctively transatlantic drawl.

'Oh no, not at all,' replied Dani, half fibbing. 'He's a friend actually . . . a "buddy" . . . But he always makes fun of me if he sees another man chatting me up.'

'Must happen all the time,' observed the handsome tennis player. 'A beautiful woman like you must always be surrounded by men.'

'Thanks . . .' Dani felt herself blushing and inwardly cursed it, aware that Mitch was still watching. 'But it doesn't happen all *that* often.'

'Maybe we could do something about that,' murmured Jamie, his voice soft but loaded with meaning. 'Have a drink or something? Maybe dinner?'

'You're very kind.' Dani shuffled the registration cards evasively. The American's interest was definitely flattering, and not, in all honesty, unwelcome, but Mitch was making her feel nervy.

Also, in the last minute or so, Reception had suddenly become very crowded. Several guests were milling around near the desk, and all were clearly seeking attention. Chief amongst them was a rather content-looking Mrs Lovingood, accompanied by the delectable and ever-present Ross. They were obviously fresh from their bed, *and* from each other, and Dani couldn't help remembering the glade.

Pandora Barrie was much in evidence too. The authoress's dreamy eyes were twinkling this morning, and she couldn't seem to keep them off Mitch. For the umpteenth time, Dani found herself wondering exactly what had happened yesterday when Mitch had gone to mend the writer's shower.

Most worrying of all, though, was the deceptively casual presence of Dani's 'prime suspect' – Perry McFadden, the eminent businessman. He was leafing through pamphlets on local points of interest, but his attention kept flicking towards the Reception desk, and especially towards Dani and Jamie.

It was really the worst time to be hob-nobbing with one guest in particular, but the handsome blond tennis player was so charming, and so thoroughly masculine and attractive, that she found it impossible to shoo him away. Having only ever seen him on television before, Dani had seriously underestimated his impact. He had an open and truly marvellous smile, shoulder-length tousled blond hair, and a genuine Californian tan. Not to mention the physique of a world-class athlete.

'How about it?' he persisted, his eyes like smouldering blue coals.

'I'm sorry,' murmured Dani, discreetly eyeing the guests all around them, and wondering if anyone was listening. 'But I really can't talk now, Mister Rivera . . .' She let her voice drop almost to a whisper, 'I'm not supposed to "fraternise" with guests, but . . . perhaps we could have a chat or something later?'

Jamie grinned – quite deliciously, Dani had to

admit – and replied with a hushed, 'You got it!'

He seemed just about to say something else – pay her an extravagant compliment, Dani hoped – when Mitch slid noiselessly behind the counter and began rearranging some just-delivered post.

'Naughty, naughty,' he breathed as he shuffled the letters. 'Did I hear talk of "fraternisation"? I thought you were teaming up with *me*?'

The words were inaudible to anyone other than Dani, but even so she kicked out sideways at her tormentor, whilst still trying to smile normally at Jamie. The tennis star returned the smile, mimed 'See you later', and strolled away, only to be replaced by yet another guest.

Dani was burning to tell Mitch to shut up and mind his own business, but a moment or two later Pandora Barrie was at the front of the queue, and gazing at him with eyes full of heat.

'Any post for me, Mitch?' the authoress purred.

Dani was shocked by the other woman's confidence. Pandora had seemed quite a shy thing yesterday, so it was clear that something radical had changed her. And judging by the smugly satisfied expression on her face whenever she looked at Mitch, *he* was the one who'd done the changing.

'Loads,' he replied, handing over a fat sheaf of letters and cards. 'Adoring fan mail, literary plaudits, and million-dollar contracts, I suppose?' He smiled warmly, and Dani watched in astonishment as his fingers slid lingering over Pandora's. It looked almost as if he were about to lift that slim white hand to his lips and smother it with passionate kisses.

'Oh yeah,' mocked Dani, presently, as Pandora sidled away with her letters then paused to look back again at Mitch. 'Now who's fraternising?'

Mitch replied with a wide-eyed 'who me?' of innocence, and continued shuffling unnecessarily through the mail.

'Just trying to improve customer relations, my sweet,' he said, peering archly over the top of his glasses. 'Which is pretty important just now, I'd've thought . . . We'll need the guests on *our* side when the axe falls.'

'Ah, so it was "customer relations" that took two hours yesterday?' Dani nodded in the direction of Pandora who'd settled down on a leather-covered banquette, ostensibly to read her correspondence. 'I'll bet there wasn't a single damn thing wrong with that shower of hers!'

'She had a problem that she couldn't solve herself . . . She needed some help,' murmured Mitch, his voice vague yet strangely serious.

Dani looked round sharply. He wasn't joking any more, she realised, and *that* troubled her more than ever. What on earth had happened between him and Pandora Barrie? she wondered, horrified by a sudden burst of pain. He'd gone upstairs and made love to another woman just after he'd finished touching *her* . . .

Swine! she thought, smiling sweetly at Mrs Lovingood, who was asking for details of local antique markets.

Bloody philandering swine, I'll kill you! she railed silently, cursing Mitch where he stood as she picked up a helpful factsheet and drew Mrs Lovingood's attention to several likely sources of collectibles.

The next few minutes were extremely busy. The guests, having finished their breakfasts, were all on the lookout for diversion. It took both Dani and Mitch to deal with all the questions, and for her part Dani was glad to be kept fully occupied.

119

All her thoughts and feelings were confused, and she didn't want even so much as a second to dwell on their content.

Why am I jealous? she asked herself at last, when the coast had cleared and Mitch had been called away.

She didn't *want* to be jealous, that was certain. And if she was, she certainly didn't want Mitch to know it. They'd said they were going to work together on the mystery, but she still couldn't define what she felt for him. Mitch was infuriating, unfathomable, and unequivocally sexually alluring . . . but did she actually *like* him? For the life of her, she still couldn't be sure.

At mid-morning break time, Dani found it hard to keep her face straight with Lois. Just as she'd imagined Mrs Lovingood in the throes of passion, she now found it hard not to picture the Assistant Manager *in flagrante delicto* as well. Visions of Lois naked and being pleasured undermined her usual air of authority, and Dani couldn't help herself grinning.

'What on earth's got into you this morning?' the blonde woman demanded, a flush across her beautifully made-up cheeks.

It's as if she knows I know, thought Dani, muttering her excuses then beating a retreat towards the small staff sitting-room. She knows and the idea of it excites her.

In the sitting-room, Dani found Cass posed cross-legged on the sofa, sipping something strange, steaming and herbal out of a battered ex-army tin cup. The gypsy girl always drank her own self-concocted beverages rather than the usual teas and coffees, and as she smelt its sharply spiced aroma Dani wondered which drink was the dodgier: Cassie's potion or the

120

water it was infused in? For her own part, Dani eyed the coffee percolator warily, then decided it was too late for the water to make a difference.

Especially when Cass looked so delectable . . .

'Come on . . .' the chambermaid said, her voice soft and wise as Dani – cup in hand – moved hesitantly towards the settee. 'We're still mates, love. I'm not going to pounce . . .' Pausing, she grinned and her dark eyes sparkled. 'Unless of course you want me to?'

'I . . . I don't know,' Dani answered, taking the seat Cass had just patted invitingly. 'I'm all mixed up . . . and worried. About the hotel, and me, and Mitch, and us, and bloody hell . . . Everything! I don't know what to do!' She took a sip of her coffee, then put the mug down with a clatter, almost spilling its contents. 'And I think Jamie Rivera fancies me now, too!'

'Cool!' exclaimed Cass.

'Not cool!' Dani replied. 'I think I've got quite enough on my plate . . . Not to mention the fact that he could well be the new owner. He's not just a pretty face, you know, he's got a whole heap of business interests as well as the tennis . . . "Hotel Aphrodisia" might be his latest deal; and if it is, he mightn't approve of me chatting up the guests.'

'I dunno,' said Cass thoughtfully. 'It might actually be your best shot.'

'Cass! Don't be an idiot! I want to get ahead legitimately . . . not by opening my legs!'

The gypsy gave her a gentle, extremely level look, then put down her mug. 'You're all strung up about this, aren't you, love?' As Dani nodded, Cass moved closer, her body warm and fragrant beneath the thin, pale cloth of her smock. 'You shouldn't worry so . . . Things will turn out all

121

right for you, I know it.' She touched her fingers lightly to her bosom. 'I feel it, Dani, truly. What will happen will happen . . . but for you it'll all work out well.'

As Cass's long fingers touched her thigh through the linen of her slim dark skirt, Dani suddenly felt mellower and calmer. 'Don't give me that "seventh daughter of a seventh daughter" nonsense,' she said with a laugh. 'You know very well I don't believe it!'

'Ah, but you do,' whispered Cass, her fingertips moving upwards, her near-black eyes hypnotic. 'You do believe in my powers . . . and you *are* tense. Why don't you let me try and relax you?'

It was clear, so clear what the Romany girl meant, and Dani couldn't help thinking of what they'd shared. All the tender, loving deliciousness that had happened when they'd returned from the bathroom. She'd not thought *more* pleasure possible, but back in her room, Cass had been as inventive and generous as before. Dani had had many, many more orgasms before she'd finally drifted off into sleep . . .

'I missed you this morning, Cassie,' she whispered, her voice faint as Cass's clever hand dipped then ascended. Dani felt it slide underneath her skirt.

'Good,' replied Cass, lifting the crisp fabric away from Dani's thighs and beginning to ease it slowly upwards. 'Would you like me to soothe away your tensions?' She paused, touching the welt of Dani's left stocking, her fingertips hovering and ready.

Dani did want it. Her body had never felt more needful of the comfort that pleasure could bring. But they were in a room that anyone could enter

. . . Mitch, Lois, someone else on the staff . . . Any one of them could come in right now and find Cass and herself making love.

'You need it, baby,' cooed Cass, anticipating her objections. 'You need what I can give you . . . and the danger will just make it all the nicer.'

To yield was pure madness, but Cass's voice was seductively smooth. Listening felt like sinking into a vat of warm honey; the words were clingy and flowing, and so sweet it was impossible to resist.

'That's it,' said Cass happily as Dani moaned in acceptance. 'Now let's make you all nice and comfy so old Cassie can help.'

Deftly, as if she'd done it a million times, Cass slid Dani's tight skirt up over her hips and rolled it into a bunch around her waist. The scrunched up fabric reminded Dani of Mitch, and the things *he'd* done to her yesterday, a memory that made her whimper and shake. She felt safe in Cass's gentle hands, but she couldn't turn off the shaming resonances. The lurid inner pictures of Mitch's long, tanned fingers on her body. The way they'd moved crudely and freely about her vulva, then violated the secrecy of her bottom with a pleasure she both resented and adored. There were memories of lunchtime as well, in the woods, when he'd played with her clitoris incessantly while they'd watched Mrs Lovingood and Ross.

'What's the matter, sweetheart?' asked Cass, resting her right hand on Dani's quaking belly. 'Has someone else been touching you?' Her deep, slanted eyes were bright and knowing. 'Has a certain talk, dark and handsome young man been making free with your body in my absence?'

Dani had pooh-poohed Cass's psychic powers

a little while ago, but in reality she tended to believe in them. Especially were sex was concerned. She hadn't told her friend the goriest details of what had happened with Mitch, but she was certain now that Cass knew everything. Everything about every last intimate crevice that Mitch had explored, and every single climax he'd inflicted. It was as if her body still bore his lustful fingerprints; the last remnants of the passion he'd created, that only someone with a special gift could see.

Someone like Cassie, who claimed she was a Romany priestess . . .

'Yes . . . Yes, he has!' cried Dani, tossing her head as Cass stroked her silky inner thighs.

'Can you show me where?' Cass asked with some gentleness, and Dani gestured vaguely at her crotch.

'No, *exactly* where,' the gypsy commanded, her voice ringing strongly now with dominance.

Dani whimpered, and said, 'No! No!', but Cass would not be gainsaid.

'Come along, my darling, let's have these panties off and we'll do it properly.'

Dani trembled all over, but Cass was already working on her briefs, skinning the thin pink lace efficiently down over her thighs, then pulling them off over her shoes.

Almost before she'd realised it, Dani found her pubis exposed. Half-stripped, she felt more wantonly provocative than she would have done if she'd been fully naked. The lingering presence of her suit, her stockings and her shoes seemed only to highlight the bareness of her sex, and she moved her bottom uneasily on the seat.

'Show me the places Mitch touched,' said Cass, sliding close and unbuttoning her smock. She

124

wore – as Dani had expected – not a single scrap of underwear beneath it, and the sight of her perfect golden body was as sweet and affecting as if it was the first time she'd unveiled it.

Dani's fears about discovery disappeared, put to flight by Cass's naked beauty. She felt her own breasts aching in her brassiere, and her clitoris throbbing wildly between her legs. She was just glad that the settee was an old one, because her juices were already dampening it.

'Show me, Dani,' Cass reiterated, sliding her hand between her own legs. 'Was it here?' she enquired, tilting her hips to show Dani her vulva, then pointing delicately at the bead of her clitoris.

'Yes,' breathed Dani, thinking of the forest then touching her own clitoris. Much as she felt anger at Mitch over a lot of things, she couldn't deny him his skills. He was an unprincipled sexual marauder, but he *had* given her pleasure, and at the time, they'd shared a state of closeness . . .

'What about here?' Cassie flicked her fingertip downwards, and circled her vaginal portal. 'Did he take you?'

'No!' It came out as a high, plaintive cry, and the regret in it shocked Dani to the core. Rubbing herself furiously, she longed to have Mitch inside her. Having him moving there . . . Thrusting strongly to bring her to pleasure. She felt orgasm rushing in towards her, and with it came another revelation.

She wanted to take *him*! She wanted to climb astride his body and ride him, control him as he'd controlled her. She imagined grinding herself down hard on his penis, and she felt a huge rush of heat in her belly as the unmistakable pulsing began. Falling sideways against Cass's naked body, she scrubbed insanely at her burning, coming pussy and groaned happily in an ecstasy of relief.

As the last lovely wave died away, Dani became aware that Cass was jerking now, her bare legs open and flailing as she rubbed like a crazy thing between them. Without thinking, Dani embraced her friend tenderly, and held her close to her heart as she came.

'Lois will go apeshit if she finds us,' observed Cass a little later as she buttoned up her smock.

Dani – still feeling shell-shocked – was tidying her hair at the room's tiny mirror. When she peered at her reflection, she was surprised by how calm and unruffled she appeared. Her make-up was just as it had looked when she'd put it on, and to her astonishment she wasn't even flushed. There was no sign whatsoever that she'd just made love, no evidence that her pretty silk and lace knickers were now in Cass's smock pocket, firmly confiscated when Dani had reached for them.

'You're probably right,' she replied, thinking of how petty Lois could be. And there was nothing more likely to irritate her than discovering that her latest lover had been playing with someone else. It was something Dani could easily sympathise with . . . She was still niggled over Pandora and Mitch.

'Not a problem now though,' said Cass brightly, twirling on the spot. 'Perfectly demure . . . "Butter wouldn't melt" . . . I'll just do my hair and I'm set.' Dani watched in admiration as Cass appeared to perform magic on her hair. Deftly manipulating her fluffy black dreads, she twisted them, then twisted again, and in two shakes had a coiled, sensuous topknot that seemed to stay up without benefit of pins.

'I don't know how you do that,' observed Dani, who could manage her own long hair quite adequately, but still envied her friend's clever tricks.

'Gypsy sleight of hand, my love,' replied Cass, making her voice sound foreign and mysterious. 'Now have we any more thoughts on the new owner?'

'No, not really,' said Dani, aware that she'd almost forgotten their dilemma. 'Perry McFadden's still the favourite . . . Although it could just as easily be Jamie. He does seem to be taking a particular interest in *me*, and I'm the one who's getting faxes.'

'He's interested in you 'cos you're gorgeous, love,' murmured Cass, coming around behind Dani and reaching down to cup the globes of her bottom. 'Imagine, the next time he comes hanging around the desk like a love-lorn puppy . . . Just think how he'd react if he knew you had no knickers on . . . and that your sweet little pussy was all hot and sticky from being pleasured by that nasty old chambermaid?'

'Cass! Be serious a minute! Our jobs are on the line . . . I know you don't care two pins where *you* work, but I like it here!'

'I'm sorry,' said Cass looking into the mirror at Dani's reflection, her expression contrite. 'You're right. I should take this more seriously.' Patting Dani very lightly on the rump, she squared her shoulders and moved away. 'I've been keeping an eye open as I clean up, but maybe I'll snoop a bit more closely from now on.'

'Don't get into trouble,' said Dani, alarmed.

'Don't you worry about that, my love,' Cass assured her as they left the sitting-room, their extended break finally over. 'Subterfuge is second nature to me, you know. I come from a nefarious background . . . and I never was one for law and order!'

Dani smiled, but she couldn't help worrying.

Back on the desk, some twenty minutes later, Dani could still hear Lois's invective. The Assistant Manager had been – justifiably – furious over her prolonged stint on the desk, and Cass appearing in Reception at the same time as Dani had only exacerbated matters. The gypsy had grinned insolently at Lois, and licked her lips suggestively, and though Dani wasn't quite sure what effect that had had on Lois, it'd certainly made *her* feel warm! She was just indulging in a harmless, distracting little fantasy when from the inner office the fax sounded its distinctive, incoming squawk.

Rushing to it, Dani yanked off the message almost before it was finished. It was a longish transmission – two sheets, one with an image – and when she looked down at what had been printed, her stomach lurched and flipped in abject horror. Her worst fears were vindicated, and then some. The text itself was minimal, but the picture that accompanied it spoke volumes.

Beneath the ominous MJK logo, the salutation and the message were familiar.

Hello again, Dani, it said. *I see I haven't fazed you in the slightest . . . Still game for a little 'fraternisation', are you? It's obvious you enjoy taking risks . . .*

Again, there was no signature, but Dani hardly noticed its absence. She was too busy gaping, in total panic, at the grainy but familiar reproduction.

She remembered that particular photoshoot very clearly. It had been her best one ever, and done for a reasonably classy magazine – a top-shelfer but with a big circulation. Her hair had been short then, and her make-up a little less subtle, but her body had been essentially the same. Just sleekening out after the tail-end of puppy-fat.

It had been an easy way to make money, and she'd never really thought of the consequences. There hadn't *been* any until now . . . There was virtually nothing to connect her to her past as a nude model; the men who bought the magazines never looked at the girls' faces anyway, and though her body was undeniably desirable, it was just one voluptuous shape among hundreds.

But now 'MJK' had discovered her secret, and something told Dani that he – or still, possibly, 'she' – wouldn't want an ex-centrefold in his luxury hotel.

'Who the devil are you, you bastard!' she whispered, eyeing the fax and trying to remember who'd mentioned 'fraternisation' recently.

Jamie Rivera soared to the top of the hitlist. She'd used that word to him herself, and he *had* already been seeking her out.

Reluctantly, she considered what she knew.

At twenty-six, Jamie Rivera was one of the world's highest paid sportsmen, and even though his on-court manner was jokey, he was known to be a master tactician. His adversaries had often been lulled into a false sense of security by his seemingly off-hand approach to the game, then minutes later been stunned when the clown turned killer.

Dani shuddered. He probably used the same strategy off court too – in his personal life, and in his business dealings. He was reputed to be a millionaire several times over, and nobody accumulated that kind of money by being Mister Nice Guy! She pictured his glinting blue eyes, then imagined them icy and calculating. The result chilled her right to her marrow, especially as she'd promised to see him later.

The rest of the morning passed quietly. There was no Mitch, no Cass, no Lois and thankfully no further sign of Jamie. Setting half her mind on auto, Dani answered calls, calculated bills and filled in laundry returns, and at the same time brooded deeply on her secret. Her secrets . . . Here she was discussing the weather with a passing guest, a retired Member of Parliament, and all the while she had a picture of her naked body in her pocket, and beneath her skirt she wasn't wearing any panties. And to cap it all some fiendiesh Machiavelli had her constantly under covert surveillance . . .

By lunchtime she was thoroughly wound up, and when Mitch turned up to take over, she frowned like thunder.

'What have I done?' he demanded, flicking pages in the Register as she got ready to leave.

'You know what you've done,' answered Dani evenly, trying not to get either riled or aroused by him. Both were almost impossible to avoid, but the second especially so, because he looked so cute and desirable in his uniform.

Some men would have looked ridiculous in the bow tie and waistcoat of a reception clerk, but unfortunately Mitch looked masculine and delicious. His pristine white shirt set off the tan of his skin to perfection, and it was amazing how what was probably a fairly cheap outfit managed to look a million dollars on him. The swine!

'What?' he persisted.

'Making stupid remarks about fraternisation . . .'

130

'Sorry,' he said sheepishly, peering over the top of his glasses, a mannerism she found particularly engaging.

'I should think so!' It was difficult to be stern with someone she fancied so much. She remembered how outrageous his hands could be, and saw again the naked beauty of his sex . . .

'I'm sorry to snarl, Mitch. But . . .' She bit her lip, reminded of the picture in her pocket. 'He's really on our case now, you know.'

'What do you mean?' Mitch's brown eyes were suddenly grave.

'I've had another fax.'

'Oh shit! You'd better show me.'

'I can't.' He'd seen almost all of her in the forest, but this was different. The pin-up wasn't sleazy or tacky, but it *was* commercial. Tantamount to selling herself sexually for money.

'Why not?' he persisted, holding out his long, elegant hand for the fax. 'Two heads are better than one, Dani. There might be a clue in the wording.'

'Because the second sheet has something very personal on it,' she said quietly.

'Then tear that bit off,' he suggested practically.

Turning away, Dani slid the fax out of her pocket, tore off the photo half as neatly as she could and handed the remainder to Mitch.

'I can see why you're worried,' he commented softly, 'but what does he, or she, mean by "taking risks"?'

Dani made a split-second decision. Knowing it was probably the stupidest thing she'd ever done, she unfolded the rest of the fax and passed it across.

Mitch stared long and intently at the grey, gritty image, adjusting his glasses again as he did

131

so. There was something so totally absorbed about the way he stared at it, so hypnotised almost, that Dani felt the real body it depicted grow hot.

'You're beautiful, Dani,' Mitch whispered after a moment, touching his fingers to the shiny fax paper. 'And even more so now . . .' As he spoke he slid his fingertip reverently over her likeness, lingering at her breasts, then moving down to her crotch.

Beneath her skirt, Dani felt the living flesh respond yet again. Her vulva grew shivery and moist, just as if he really were caressing it, and her clitoris pulsed slowly at its heart.

As if he sensed what his presence was doing, Mitch turned to her, his eyes big and dark behind his glasses. 'I—' he began, but at that second the house phone beside him rang shrilly.

With a black frown he picked it up and said 'Yes?'

While Mitch reached for a pencil and notepad, Dani was able to snatch back the incriminating picture. She was only half listening to the one-sided conversation, but as Mitch began scribbling on the pad she could see it was instructions for a guest's light lunch – to be served on a trolley in their room.

'Buck's Fizz? Certainly, sir,' said Mitch silkily, while at the same time narrowing his eyes and pulling a face. 'Yes . . . Of course. I'll see if she's available. Either way, we'll have your lunch ready for you in five or ten minutes. Thank you, sir.'

Putting the phone down, Mitch made a moue of distaste, then tapped his notepad. 'Rivera,' he said dismissively. 'Wanting Buck's Fizz, crudités and cold chicken . . . To be served by your own good self, Ms Stratton. Do you think he's the one

who sent that?' He nodded at what was left of the fax.

For a moment, Dani thought of a Wimbledon semi-final when Jamie had totally bamboozled his opponent with the most demonic of tactics, and then she nodded. 'He could well be,' she said pensively. 'But what on earth does he want *me* for?'

Almost before the words were out, Mitch took her by the arm and made her face him. 'Good God, Dani, he's a man and he's breathing,' he hissed, his face taut, his mouth vehement, and his dark brows a hard, expressive line. 'With *you* he doesn't need another reason!'

The ferocity in Mitch's voice was shocking, and seemed to pass through Dani's body like a wave. She felt it crest between her legs, where her hot sex longed for him, and realised that this handsome, aggravating and dangerous man really did feel something genuine for her, something more than just a persistent urge to tease. The heat in his eyes seemed to burn her, magnified by the lenses of his glasses, and his pressing fingers hurt her upper arm. His grip was like a spring-driven pincer, his hold on her totally unbreakable.

'I won't go then,' she said defiantly. 'I'm not a call girl . . . He can't just summon me!'

Still caught in his man-of-steel grip, Dani watched Mitch's face with fascination. A gamut of emotions seemed to parade across his strong, chiselled features, as if he were weighing up a dozen possibilities.

'You've got to go,' he said finally, seeming to calm down as he released her tingling arm. 'This is the ideal opportunity to find out about him . . . You might even be able to manoeuvre him into an admission. If *you* can't do it, nobody can.'

He was right, she knew it. And he knew it, even if he seemed not to like it. Jamie Rivera had been drawn to her, and didn't all men like boasting of their power in the presence of a woman who was available? Or who *appeared* to be available.

'Okay, I'll do it,' she said, still troubled.

Jamie Rivera was a glamorous, magnetic man ... What would happen in the heat of the moment if appearances suddenly *weren't* deceptive?

10 Advantage, Ms Stratton

DANI LOVED BUCK'S Fizz, but as she wheeled the laden trolley out of the lift, she eyed the tall, half-filled jug of orange juice warily. In it was a cluster of floating ice-cubes. Melting ice cubes, made from Bouvier Manor water . . .

'Somehow, I don't think you need it, Mister Rivera,' she whispered as she hovered before the door, then reached out and tentatively knocked.

After a moment, the door swung open, and the greeting on her lips died abruptly. Standing in the open doorway was a very famous body, virtually naked. Only a small monogrammed towel covered the smiling, dripping Jamie.

'Boy, that was quick!' he exclaimed, stepping backwards to let her pass. 'I thought I'd have time to grab a shower *and* get dressed. This sure is a great place for service!'

Dogged by her suspicions, Dani wondered if this was some kind of challenge. 'Would you like me to stay and set out your meal, sir?' she asked primly, feeling far less cool and assured than she had done when they'd chatted in Reception.

'Hey, why so formal?' asked Jamie. He moved quickly towards her, then stopped short again, his tiny towel slipping. Athlete or no, his reflexes weren't quite fast enough and the makeshift garment fell apart, leaving Jamie clutching it modestly to his privates, but with his trim golden backside on show.

'Oops,' he said mischievously, and Dani noted he made little attempt to cover himself. 'I think I'd better put some clothes on. Why don't you mix us both some Fizz while I dress?' With that he strolled unhurriedly from the room, his firm buttocks still unadorned.

They're all the same! thought Dani, gritting her teeth. He thinks all he has to do is show me his gorgeous bum and I'm helpless!

The trouble was, the sight of Jamie's tight male rump *had* affected her. That, and the way his muscles rippled strongly as he walked.

'Chauvinist bastard!' she muttered as she slowly teased out the champagne cork and thought how similar Mitch and Jamie were. Both so anxious to flaunt their physiques . . .

And they do it so well, she admitted, mixing the Buck's Fizz with some flair, then turning her attention to the arrangement of the food.

The lunch was simple, and admirably healthy, and only took a moment to set out. When it was served and ready, Dani decided it was time for a little discreet and very cautious snooping.

There was certainly plenty to suggest that Jamie Rivera was her quarry. As well as the obvious sports gear, there was an open attaché case on the sofa, a copy of the *Financial Times*, and even the ubiquitous laptop computer on the writing desk. Most incriminating of all was a miniature modem – not connected at the moment – but certainly capable of transmitting a fax if required.

Stepping towards the case, Dani shot a wary

glance towards the bathroom. The door was slightly ajar and she could see Jamie's moving shadow in the room beyond, as presumably he dried his wet body. She could hear the swish of the towel, various 'grooming' sounds, and – quite endearingly – some very loud and off-key whistling. He sounded relaxed and utterly contented, and if he was deceiving her, he was doing it beautifully.

Sensing she still had a couple of minutes, Dani concentrated her efforts on the briefcase. There were quite a lot of documents in it, but a quick flick through revealed no hint of what she was seeking. There were share reports, bank statements, and what looked like the draft contract for a lucrative new sponsorship deal, but nothing, not a single line, about the purchase of a luxury hotel.

Dani searched in silence, but as she fished in to get the last of the folders, a sound from the bathroom made her fumble, and to her horror the case slewed sideways. Catching it neatly, she discovered the source of the instability. The case was sitting on top of a thick wedge of magazines, and their glossy covers had caused it to slide.

Unfortunately the magazines weren't as catchable as the case, and the whole lot went slithering to the carpet. Dani got brief, eye-widening glimpses of their contents as she did her best to gather them quickly, but dropped the whole lot again in an instant as a strong hand reached out to assist her.

'Got a problem?' enquired Jamie, his soft voice suddenly sounding threatening.

Dani was dumbfounded, but at the same time her mind worked with elegance. Analysing Jamie's tone, she detected more fear than actual anger, and when she looked more closely at the magazines, she could clearly determine its cause. Jamie Rivera had at least as much to hide as she did, a fact which restored her composure.

'No, it's all right,' she answered smoothly. 'I've decided to stay for that drink you offered. I was just making a space to sit down.'

'Great,' said Jamie, still sounding faintly nervous as he grabbed up the magazines and the briefcase, then stuffed the whole lot to one side in a chair. As Dani sat down in the place he'd cleared, he took the jug of Fizz and the glasses from the trolley, then placed them on a coffee table close by.

Yes, it *is* rather great! thought Dani, allowing Jamie Rivera, one of the world's most handsome and flamboyant sports stars, to wait on her. As he handed her a tall glass of Fizz, she realised – with a frisson of delight – that the magazines had given her the advantage. Jamie should have been laid back and completely in his element by now, but he wasn't. He looked magnificent – his gilded muscularity was perfectly flattered by a white cropped top and matching thin, loose shorts – but one glimpse of his dark, secret preferences had handed Dani the situation on a plate.

'Cheers!' she said softly, clinking her glass to his, and letting her eyes run assessingly over him.

Jamie Rivera was certainly a glorious piece of work, and even hunkier at very close quarters. His sunstreaked blond hair was caught back in a tail, and his compact, athletic body was lightly tanned wherever she could see it. This smooth, all encompassing sheen was accentuated by his skimpy white clothing, and the loose, gaping cutaways of his vest displayed the breadth of his shoulders to perfection.

His shorts showed off other things too. There was a clearly defined bulge at the vee of his groin – and it was beginning to grow before Dani's ogling eyes!

Returning her salutation, her host drank deeply, then put his empty glass down on the coffee table. His obvious need for alcohol made Dani feel even more confident. She increased the knowing brilliance of her smile.

'So, here we are,' she said brightly, crossing her legs, but remembering to take special care. Her knickers were still in Cass's pocket. 'Just think . . . there must be millions of girls who'd like to be me right now. All alone with Jamie Rivera. In his bedroom, and privy to his intimate secrets.'

Jamie drew a deep breath, then grinned resignedly.

'Okay, so you found my magazines,' he said, shrugging his imposing shoulders, 'and I admit it. I'm like ninety-nine point nine of all the guys on this earth . . . I'm some kind of pervert.' Reaching for the Fizz jug, he poured himself another long shot, then nodded towards Dani's glass.

Dani shook her head, then eyed him squarely. 'Everyone's got something to hide,' she murmured, wondering if there was a way to trade with him over this, a way of using this interesting new knowledge. Blackmail was an ugly concept, but if he *did* own the hotel, she needed any and every lever she could find.

Jamie drank again, more slowly this time. 'Do you want to make something of this, Dani,' he said, meeting her eyes over the top of his glass. 'You could easily sell the story to a newspaper.' He placed the glass down again, his knuckles slightly whitened. 'I'm good copy. Some tabloid rag would love all this . . .' He gestured vaguely in the direction of the magazines, his face smiling but his blue eyes grim.

Dani paused, getting a thrill from Jamie's obvious tension. He was trying to act cool, but it was clear he *was* bothered. There were scandals every week in the sports world, but Jamie Rivera had stayed relatively unscathed – until now.

'No,' she said at last. 'I've no intention of doing anything like that.' She took a drink of her Fizz, and studied Jamie's smile of relief. 'But there is one thing I'd like from you.'

The haunted look returned – so suddenly and dramatically that Dani felt a stab of arousal. The sensation of having such a charismatic man on the end of a string was intoxicating, and it rushed through her loins like a heatstorm.

'What's that?' he asked.

'The answer to a question,' Dani answered, keeping her voice level and bland.

'Which is?'

Again, she paused, this time trying to gauge whether Jamie actually knew what the question was. His handsome face was puzzled, yet open. Was he really in the dark or just a consummate bluffer?

'Do you own this hotel?' she asked finally, tucking her crossed fingers under her thigh.

Jamie frowned, then smiled, his surprise unfeigned. 'No ... No, I don't,' he said, smoothing his hand over his casually bound hair, and still looking genuinely befuddled. 'But I'm beginning to wish I did,' he added, his blue eyes regaining their mischief.

A strange mix of emotions hit Dani as Jamie recovered his poise. She'd miscalculated, she realised. Blown it completely. This man could probably get her sacked now, but instead of feeling scared she felt elated. And excited in the most sensuous of ways.

Jamie's smile broadened into his world-famous boyish grin, an expression well known from his tennis court triumphs. He was winning here too, and he knew it.

'It doesn't make a lot of difference, actually,' Dani observed, taking a long sip of her drink. 'You don't have to own the place to get me dismissed.'

'Why would I want to do that?' he asked, mocking her with innocence.

'I . . .'

To admit to the game would be to admit guilt, and Dani felt her face colour and her heart start to pound. So much for sleuthing, for taking control. This man was an experienced career tactician – how the devil could *she* score any points?

'Look, Dani, this is all down to me,' said Jamie, suddenly and unexpectedly reasonable, '*I* invited you to my room. *I'm* the one who plied you with drink . . . You're not the guilty one.' He looked her straight in the eye. 'It's *me* who deserves to be punished.'

For a moment, Dani lost track of things, as if she'd dropped into a play with no script. Jamie was giving her a hint of some kind, but she felt stuck with a bad case of brain lag.

At that moment, as if by magic intervention, the precarious heap of magazines started slithering en masse to the floor. Distracted, Dani looked across, then as one of them flipped open at a double page spread, her doubts cleared like mist in the sun.

Well, most of them . . . There was just one thing that *still* didn't gel.

Making an adjustment to her skirt, Dani rose to

her feet and walked across to the fallen magazines. Picking one up, she studied his esoteric content for a moment, then smiled. She'd never actually done what was shown in the photo – not for real – but she'd simulated it in her days as a model.

'You're into this, aren't you?' she asked mildly, returning to her place beside Jamie and spreading the magazine across both their laps.

'I'm afraid so,' he said ruefully, looking downwards at the large, coloured pictures.

Some years ago, at the lowest struggling depths of her modelling career, Dani had posed for specialised 'spanking' magazines. She'd appeared in a variety of ludicrous photostories, and each time played a similar type of role. A naughty secretary. A naughty schoolgirl. A naughty housemaid. The tacky, poorly-made costumes had been different in the initial stages, but the endpiece had always been the same – herself, face down and bare-bottomed, spread across a variety of chairs, tables and desks. Or alternatively across knees, either male or female. She'd never actually *been* spanked, but often, on seeing the finished product, she'd found herself wishing the deed had been done. At the time of being photographed, she'd felt nothing, yet the images themselves – then *and* now – had definitely turned her on.

The pictures in Jamie's magazines were superb. Fetish was fashion these days, and projected with glamour at no expense spared, but the subject itself was essentially the same as in the tacky magazines from her past. Naked bottoms and thighs being punished with hands, straps and canes . . .

And if this was Jamie's peccadillo, Dani could

see a way clear of her dilemma. A deal could be struck. She could get out of this room with her job still intact . . . even if her body had to suffer in the process.

'Have you ever done it for real?' she ventured, turning a page with great care and mentally re-crossing her fingers. This was a delicate juncture, and to offer herself too bluntly would be worse than not offering at all.

'No . . . No, I haven't,' answered Jamie, his voice soft and taught, as if he were also treading a tightrope. 'I've wanted to . . . Often. But it's back to that dilemma again. Being a public person the press could destroy.'

'What if someone could help you?' Dani postulated, running a fingertip over the image of a woman's pale, naked hindquarters. The model was across the knee of another woman, and her lavender silk drawers were crumpled in a pool around her ankles. 'Someone who wouldn't say anything to anybody, if you didn't say anything about her?' She looked up and focused on Jamie, locking her eyes with the blue fire in his.

'I think I'd be very tempted,' he said, looking down again at the picture, then pursing his lips, 'I think I'd say "yes" . . . But I'd have to tell this person something first. Something she mightn't like, because it wasn't precisely what she'd had in mind.' As he spoke, he shuffled uncomfortably on the sofa.

Dani eased the magazine forward ever-so-slightly and studied the disturbance in Jamie's snowy shorts. He was clearly erect, and ready for their game, and in a flash of illuminating insight, Dani finally understood *what* it was. *Exactly* what it was.

'Oh my,' she said quietly, 'you are a naughty

143

boy, aren't you?' She paused, ran her fingers over the magazine, then let them stray on to the bronzed leg it lay across. 'Fancy wanting that? It seems to me if you *want* something like that, you jolly well *deserve* it!'

The leg beneath her fingertips quivered finely, and she sensed great happiness in the man at her side. What must it feel like, she wondered, to know that at any second your most cherished and decadent fantasy would come true? Just thinking about it made her sex pout and moisten, and it wasn't even her dream . . . Whatever was it doing to Jamie?

Her only remaining qualm, as she turned another page, was that her performance might not satisfy him. She'd never been spanked, and she'd never spanked anyone herself . . . Could she be stern? Could she be dominant? Could she hit with enough vigour and force? There was only one way to find out.

'Jamie, will you stand up, please?' she said, shaping her voice into schoolma'amish tone.

The darling of the world's tennis courts rose hesitantly to his feet, his eyes downcast and his demeanour meek and respectful. For all the role she was about to assume, Dani felt the deepest of respect for Jamie . . . Not many men would be able to cede their machismo like this. Mitch certainly wouldn't do it, damn him, and in her eyes he *needed* some punishment!

'Now, James,' continued Dani, finding formality seemed to make things easier. 'You've been reading some very unpleasant literature recently. Magazines that are quite unsuitable for a well-brought-up young gentleman. There's really no excuse for such wickedness. Have you anything to say in your defence?'

Jamie's long eyelashes fluttered, and he nibbled his trembling lower lip. Dani was utterly fascinated by the change in him. He'd gone from confident adult maleness to abject juvenile submission in the space of a handful of seconds . . . How long had he been planning this scenario? How many times had he played it out in his mind, then taken hold of his penis?

'Answer me, boy!' she hissed, rising to her feet and beginning to pace to and fro. 'Tell me all about this disgusting habit of yours, James. Tell me how often you read these filthy magazines . . . and what unspeakable things you do when you've read them.'

Jamie was in raptures. His face was fire-pink beneath his tan, his eyes were closed, and he was panting heavily. In his shorts, his penis was rampant, pushing out the white cloth at his crotch.

'You revolt me, Rivera,' Dani said richly, the thwarted actress in her thrilling to the role. She found herself thinking of Mitch again, imagining him in Jamie's place and waiting for the sting of her hand. Boy, would she make *him* suffer!

'You're a repulsive, undisciplined little worm,' she went on, with high enthusiasm. 'Insulting me with a gross display like that—' She let the back of her hand brush Jamie's hardness, and was rewarded by a low, plaintive moan, and the sway of his hips towards her. 'Don't you have any self-control at all?'

Jamie didn't answer, so Dani went on, imperiously, 'And you're bad mannered too. Not answering a simple question when it's put to you. That's another misdemeanour to be punished.'

Thoroughly enjoying herself, Dani returned to her place on the settee. It was peculiar how these

145

ritualistic preliminaries were as arousing as any conventional foreplay. Between her legs, the folds of her sex were throbbing with a slow, drumlike beat, and if she had been wearing any knickers they'd have been thoroughly sticky by now. She felt as if she were a bottle of shaken champagne, her erotic heart bubbling with readiness and on the point of effervescing any second. She was bursting with a raw need to touch herself, but even so, she managed to hold fast.

'Do I not get an answer?' she enquired archly, her eyes on Jamie's pinkened, downcast face.

'Yes . . . I . . .'

' "Yes, Ms Stratton",' she prompted, 'and I'd prefer it if you looked at me when I'm talking to you.'

'Yes, Ms Stratton,' he answered in a faint, barely audible voice.

'Yes, what? I still haven't heard a confession.'

'I read the magazines often, Ms Stratton,' he whispered, his fists clenched his sides. 'I read them, then I touch myself.'

'Which part of your body do you touch?'

'My prick.'

' "Prick"! Good grief, Rivera, what kind of language is that to use in front of me? I'm afraid you'll have to pay for that.'

It was getting harder and harder to contain herself. Dani sat quite still on the settee, with her legs elegantly crossed and her hands clasped lightly on her knee, but inside her body was ablaze. If she pressed her thighs together, and squeezed her inner muscles, she knew she'd have an orgasm, and in the cradling lace of her bra, her nipples felt ready to burst. Under normal circumstances, she'd have been spread across the bed by now, with Jamie hard at work between her

146

legs. But these weren't normal circumstances . . . and Jamie wanted to be *over* her legs, not between them.

'I'm . . . I'm sorry, Ms Stratton,' he apologised, still faltering.

'So describe.'

'I take my magazines to bed with me. And when I've looked at them long enough, I unfasten my shorts, uncover my penis and stroke it with my fingers till I come . . .'

A pretty picture, thought Dani, really wishing she could be around to see it.

'Loathsome,' she lied. 'Completely vile and disgusting. I can't tolerate such unsavoury habits.'

There was a dark stain on the front of Jamie's shorts now, where his penis wept silky tears of joy. Dani decided it was high time she saw it naked.

'You may lower your shorts now, James.' Her voice was calm and low, although her heartbeat and body were in turmoil. 'Come along . . . Get a move on . . . I don't have all day,' she said more sternly when Jamie seemed frozen.

After a couple of deep breaths, he settled his hands on his waistband, his fingers clearly shaking. He took another breath, then eased the garment slowly down his hips and thighs, and gasped when his penis leapt free of it, untrammelled by any kind of underwear.

'That's far enough,' instructed Dani when the shorts were caught at Jamie's knees. With an expression of utter desperation, he had to spread his golden thighs to stop them slipping.

She said nothing more for several seconds. Then several more, extending the hiatus into a full, agonising minute. Jamie's erect prick swayed

147

gently in time to the quivers that wracked his whole body, but Dani couldn't imagine it staying so very hard for much longer. He was too excited. He'd come the instant she touched him.

Even so, there was a game to play. 'Miss and Pupil' or some other dour relationship like that. 'You'd better get yourself across my lap then, hadn't you?' she said, making her voice sound bored and weary, and her body language cool and aloof. In her heart, she knew she wasn't fooling him at all – her cheeks were flushed, and she was certain her eyes were bright as stars – but at least she was *trying* to fake it and reproduce the severity he longed for.

Surprisingly, Jamie did not lose control when he touched her, and he took his place with a modicum of grace. His golden brown buttocks were taut and she could feel his sex like a poker against her thigh, but despite this he kept his body quite still. He even remained motionless when she touched the tips of her fingers to each bottom-cheek, testing the resilience of his firm, manly flesh.

Jamie's rump was truly a thing of beauty: tanned, almost sculpted, and as hard and gleaming as oak. Dani wondered how many times she'd seen him lunge across the court and save an impossible shot, propelled by these marvellous muscles. Exploring the shape of him, she breathed deeply, drawing in the aroma of his citrus cologne and the smell of his fear and excitement.

It's now or never, she thought, lifting her hand and – before she could change her mind – bringing it down on his quivering right cheek.

The sound the smack made was astonishing, far louder than she'd ever imagined. Had she hit him too hard, she wondered. He hadn't cried out or protested though, so maybe it hadn't been enough?

She smacked the left cheek for comparison, and watched it bounce, whiten briefly, then begin to colour up a livid cherry pink.

Her victim still made no sound, nor did he wriggle or struggle. He was immobile in her lap, yet his prick was like an iron bar against her. The only indication at all of his feelings was an increase in the depth of his breathing.

How could he remain so controlled? For her own part, Dani was getting more and more aroused by the second, and just two blows had brought her close to the edge. She wondered if Jamie could feel *her* heat as it rose through the linen of her skirt. Perhaps he could smell her too? She was wet now, a silvery, sexual gooeyness in the niche between her thighs. It's odour would be ripe and freshly pungent; especially to one so near the source.

Landing two more spanks, she wished she knew better what to do. She was already deeply fond of her tennis star, and wanted to please him and give him what he so obviously and desperately needed.

How many times did you have to do it? How many smacks? Where was the line between pleasure and cruelty? As she laid on one, two, three more strokes, she still wasn't quite sure about the force of them. Hesitating, she misjudged the next, and hit awkwardly, just under the hang of one cheek. The blow must've gained impact from the angle, some extra kind of speed and energy, because Jamie cried out loud and brokenly, and for the first time he squirmed on her lap.

149

'Too hard?' she asked, trying not to give away her doubts.

'No! Oh God, no!' panted Jamie, moving his penis furiously against her. 'It's beautiful . . . Oh, yes, please . . . Go on!'

So crueller was better? she thought, landing another couple of loosely aimed strikes. There was a large area of redness now, and she sensed that slaps on top of slaps were more painful, and in consequence, gave Jamie more pleasure.

But she still found it hard to really wallop. To put her full might and bodyweight behind the blows.

What if she pretended she was smacking someone else? True severity might be easier that way.

Smack! Suddenly the man in her lap wasn't Jamie at all, but Mitch, his strong body tense and slowly writhing.

You swine! thought Dani, raising her hand high and bringing it down without remorse or restraint. You bastard! Teasing me and touching me . . . Grinning, acting clever . . . Being beautiful . . . Smack! Smack! Smack! Smack! Smack!

Suddenly Jamie began mewling in distress, and his identity changed yet again. This time he was Lois, so hoity-toity, getting her come-uppance from Dani's slender hand . . .

Bitch! Take that! Dani cried silently, laying down blows with real fury. Talking down to me . . . Dismissing me . . . Being dishonest and sneering and hard . . . Her hand rained down another volley.

And then Lois became Richard, weak and despicable. Then Cass, all wicked, delicious temptation with a bottom so ripe for pain's kiss.

Pandora Barrie was next, the simpering little

flirt. She really *deserved* a good leathering. Luring Mitch to her room with false tales of malfunctioning showers.

As her hand pounded down again and again and again, Dani realised that her blows were right on target. Jamie was whimpering loudly now, and throwing himself around on her knee. His legs were kicking and straightening with each spank that landed, and the motion was rucking up her skirt. She could feel his penis pressed directly against her legs now, through the ultra-sheer silkiness of her stocking, and where he touched her, the fine nylon was soaking.

'You dirty little boy,' she said fiercely, 'You're making a mess on me!' Raising her arm high, above her head, she let fly with her most ferocious blow yet and ignored the sharp stinging in her palm.

The moment the contact was made, Jamie lifted his head and cried out. Clinging on to both her and the couch, he straightened his body, then arched again, grinding his pelvis against the line of her thigh, and caressing her rabidly with his cock. She could feel his moisture, his member leaping, and the rasp of his wiry pubic hair; and as his penis anointed her with semen, he moaned plaintively in passion and relief.

'Oh Dani! Oh Dani!' he sobbed, still coming as *she* still smacked. Each slap synchronised perfectly with a spurt of his essence, and the more she hit him, the more he seemed to throb.

And when, finally, she pressed her fingertips reverently to his burning red flesh, Jamie crooned back to her quietly and sweetly. Were his cries of pain, or of joy? She couldn't tell. She only knew she craved release for herself . . .

Nudging him gently off her lap, she guided his

body as he slithered to the floor, then kissed his face as he groaned in obvious pain. As their mouths drew apart, he looked up at her, his blue eyes bright as sapphires with gratitude . . . and a lovely, almost slavish need to please.

It took only the subtlest of signals to show him what it was she wanted, and as she lay back on the settee – her fingers at her skirt and her thighs sliding open – she felt his warm breath caress her aching sex.

11   The Waiting

MITCH HAD NEVER felt so awful in his life.

He was appalled by his reactions and stunned by his emotions, both by their power and the fact they existed at all. He'd never expected this burning rage in his belly, this sense of being devoured from inside. It was plain old-fashioned jealousy, he realised, and in his book, completely irrational.

It seemed like an aeon since Dani had disappeared with the trolley, although in fact it'd only been an hour. Even so, common sense kept reminding him unpleasantly that it didn't take *this* long to serve a lunch.

You encouraged her, you cretin! he berated himself as he stacked pallets of soft drinks and mixers in the small storeroom beside the butler's pantry. *You* told her to go up there snooping and find out anything by any means she could.

Mitch had found it easy to excuse Dani's absence twenty minutes ago, when Lois had relieved him on the desk; but he couldn't excuse it now. His mind was playing a string of monstrous tricks on him, tormenting him unrelentingly, and instead seeing the bottles and cans he was arranging, he saw only Dani in

Rivera's arms, the pair of them writhing and naked.

This wasn't what he'd planned when he'd first come to the Bouvier Manor. Not at all . . . He'd hoped for sex, definitely, and the company of beautiful women; but not a fixation with one particular woman. He would have called the feeling a 'crush' if he'd been fifteen again, but even though he knew he looked much younger than his age, he was a grown man and he'd thought he was way past such weakness.

Call yourself egalitarian, Mitchell? he demanded, trying to work out what had gone wrong. You expect total sexual freedom for yourself, so why can't you allow Dani the same? Why is it okay for you to have Pandora, and Cassie, and whoever takes your fancy, and her not have Jamie Rivera?

'Because it just bloody isn't!' he growled, sending a hunk of cardboard packaging hurtling across the room. The missile impacted harmlessly on a tall stack of crisp boxes in the corner, and Mitch wished to God he'd thrown a bottle instead.

'Just isn't bloody what?' enquired a slow husky voice from behind him. 'What the hell's making *you* so crazy?'

Mitch spun around and found Cass just behind him, her dark hair tied back in a knot of some kind and her gypsy eyes glitteringly mischievous. As ever, she had that certain, scary look of knowledge on her face, the light that seemed to shine from inside her and made him feel his every thought was transparent.

'Nothing,' he replied abruptly, aware of an instant response to Cass's beauty, a tumescence he didn't need right now. He wanted to think

154

straight, or sulk, or both, but there was something untamed about this woman that got to him every time, even though he couldn't really class her as his 'type'. She was uncivilised, and her lovemaking was ferocious. He could still feel her teeth sinking into his shoulder from the last time they'd been to bed together.

'Bollocks,' replied Cass bluntly. 'You're mad as hell about something.' Her brown-black eyes met his squarely for a second, then panned slowly down over his body, 'And from the looks of your crotch it's a woman.' Her knowing smile widened. 'It couldn't be anything to do with Dani taking a certain tennis player his lunch about an hour ago, could it? And the fact that she hasn't been seen since?

Mitch reached savagely for another box. Cass was right, of course, as she always was; but it was no comfort whatsoever to him. He was painfully aroused now, and the visions of Dani and Rivera were all mixed up with pictures of Cass herself as she'd looked when he'd pinned her underneath him. He could see her with her head thrown back and her burnished neck taut, her body bucking and arching against his and her eyes closed tightly in rapture.

'I'm jealous too, you know,' she said suddenly, sitting down on a ratty old stool that stood in the corner of the room. 'But I don't think *either* of us has a right to be.'

Mitch felt dizzy as he absorbed what she'd said. Dani and Cass? Oh God, the very thought of it made his loins turn molten . . . Two beautiful women. Two perfect bodies. Two luscious, sexual entities entwined in each others arms: touching, kissing and fondling. Fingers and tongues, and the sweet, fragrant smoothness of silken female skin. Two lovers at the pinnacle of sensation.

Cass had the only stool, but without warning Mitch's knees felt weak. The enormity of Cass and Dani being together had pole-axed him, and made him fevered with fantasies and lust. He couldn't forget that Dani might be having sex with Jamie Rivera at this very moment, but suddenly it seemed to lose all significance. He felt only the faintest of pangs.

What did they do together? he wondered. This gypsy and his sleek, feisty Dani? How did they start? Did they kiss as a man and woman would? Was one dominant and the other submissive? Or did they frolic and caress as equals?

'H . . . how long?' he stammered. 'How long have you been . . .?'

'Oh, not long,' murmured Cass, her eyes and her whole face dreamy. As he watched her, Mitch got a sudden rush of insight 'The thing' had only just happened, he realised, and Cass – usually so strong and independent – was quite desperately enamoured of her friend.

'I never knew,' he said, more confused than ever. They couldn't be exclusively lesbian, or neither one of them would have responded to *him*. And they had responded, hadn't they?

Horrible doubts assailed him. Complex suspicions, all tied up with a man's deepest fear. What if they'd been faking it, the pair of them? What if they'd been using him? Testing him? Given the situation at the hotel, and the atmosphere of distrust . . . it *was* a possibility.

'Oh my, you've gone all pale,' said Cass blithely, rising from her stool and strolling across the room, 'Poor dear Mitch,' she whispered as she stood before him, and reached out to lay her fingers against his lips. 'Don't worry. I like men

. . . And so does Dani. What happened with you wasn't put on.'

Mitch felt idiotically relieved, and his elation made him sway towards Cassie and put his arms automatically around her.

Yes! I *knew* it was real! he thought wildly, hugging her warm body against him in a spontaneous gesture of triumph. Without his waistcoat – which he'd shed because it was hot – there were no more than two layers of cloth between them. He could feel the full, soft roundness of Cass's marvellous breasts, feel them vibrant and alive against his chest. He could feel her nipples like two hard fruit pits, the twin points digging into his flesh.

Beneath her skimpy overall, he knew there was a hot, bare body, honeyed skin, and a sex that was tight yet welcoming. For a peculiar moment, it seemed that it wasn't just Cass pressed against him, but a strange, magic, dual creature that also seemed part Dani. Wild, dark Cass was still wild, dark Cass, but within her he experienced a finer beauty, a more complex yet equally powerful sexuality that spoke of a woman less direct and more cerebral.

'You want her too, don't you?' Cass growled, her mouth against his throat. 'And you want her now . . . Just as I do . . .'

He was helpless, locked tight in his desire for two women. He felt Cass adjusting herself against him, parting her long, smooth-skinned thighs around one of his and pressing her naked sex against his thin trousers. Somewhere along the line – he wasn't sure when – she'd yanked up her abbreviated overall, and laid her female core open to the air.

'Yes . . . ' He heard the ragged word, yet wasn't

quite sure if he'd spoken. His heart and his loins were saying 'yes', but clearly Cass's were too. She was working herself rhythmically against his thigh now, massaging her vulva on the hard sheaf of muscle. He could feel her thick, slippy wetness through the barrier of the cloth, feel her shape and a slow even pulse.

'Yes!' The cry came again and it was definitely Cass this time, her pleasure hot as fire as she rubbed and writhed like a jungle she-panther in season. 'Oh God, yes!' she shouted, then seemed to collapse against him, her arms around his neck and her pelvis swivelling and swirling. He looked down hungrily at the vee of her thighs, where her black hair met the blackness of his trousers. Between his own thighs, his cock was in torment.

Seeing Cass, he could also see Dani. As he pictured her lovely body in the woods, he seemed to feel the texture of her skin too – when he'd stroked her from his hide beneath the desk.

And yet, all the while, it was Cass in his arms and arousing him. Confused, he reached down and clasped the bottom of the climaxing woman, but wasn't sure who the gesture was for.

'Mmmm,' breathed Cass, still jerking, 'Yes, I like that . . . I love a man who'll fondle my bum.'

Mitch loved doing it. Locked entirely into Cass now, he let his fingertips explore her firm rump. The skin of her cheeks was as delicate as pure satin, and in the crevice, her heat was infernal. When he touched her rosebud, the tiny tight sphincter, she screamed and jammed her body against him, her new climax more frenzied than the last.

The more he stroked her, the more Cass came, and her cries echoed loudly around them. As her sweating body rocked against him, Mitch felt giddy with a strange, transferred pleasure. She was orgasming continuously, lost in the highest of ecstasies, and his own sex was aroused fit to burst. He groaned aloud at the sumptuous agony.

'Oh Jesus . . . Oh please,' he begged, barely aware of what he was saying. His penis was crushed inside his trousers, the pain exquisite and grinding. He'd never felt harder in his life.

'It's all right, baby. It's all right,' whispered Cass, sliding slowly down his torso, her own crisis now clearly over. Undulating like a houri, she inched her way gradually to the floor, then settled gracefully on her knees before him.

Mitch felt frozen. Frozen, yet in flames; and he shuddered when she reached for his groin. In seconds, she had his trousers ripped open, then his shorts, and was pulling out his long, reddened member.

'Oh, that's beautiful,' she whispered, her breath like raw flame on his flesh.

When she put out her pointed tongue, Mitch whimpered and pushed his body towards it. 'Please . . . ' he begged.

'Gladly,' said Cass, with enthusiasm, diving forward and engulfing him completely before he'd even had time to draw breath.

Her mouth was a fluid-filled cavern of warmth, perfect bliss to his sorely vexed flesh. He sighed as she let him in even deeper, doing something almost impossible with the muscles of her throat, while her fingers dove greedily into his underwear and enclosed the aching fury of his balls.

Mitch was amazed he didn't climax immediately. He'd been wanting something like this so desperately, yet now he was in Cass's mouth, and being laved by her moist, nimble tongue, he seemed to find a new level of control. The great, all-encompassing tension was still there, but it was transformed into a new, and more rarefied delight. He felt himself floating, his mind sharp and clear as if detached from his bodily sensations. He felt a peculiar, benign fondness for the woman who was sucking him, but at the same time, his thoughts yearned elsewhere. There was no conflict in fantasising about Dani, it seemed, whilst being caressed by the lips of her friend.

But would Dani also feel like this? He shuddered as Cass's tongue found a beautifully sensitive spot. Would Miss Stratton dive and probe with her tongue, would her throat open so completely and yet not gag? Would she let him climax, deep inside, and fill her velvety mouth with his come?

As his thighs began to shudder, he felt the quest inside his shorts go deeper. With a touch as gentle as the passing kiss of a moth, Cass delicately palpated his anus.

Seconds after the first sweet stroke, hot lead seemed to boil in his entrails, and with a huge cry, he grabbed Cassie's head, then pumped his hips in an uncontrolled frenzy. He was dimly aware that his actions were coarse and unheeding, but there was no way on earth he could change them. He was lost, insane, flying. A great jolt seemed to surge through his loins as he fought to keep the strength in his legs. Sobbing like a child, he felt his semen jet out, then pool around his flesh in Cass's mouth. He could hear – and feel – her gulping, and in an instant she was swallowing furiously whilst still fondling his bottom with her fingers.

By a miracle, Mitch managed to stay on his feet as he came, but as the pleasure ebbed, his knees started buckling.

'Cassie . . . ' he muttered as his penis slipped wetly from her mouth. Staggering, he moved towards the stool and slumped onto it, the zip on his trousers still undone. He felt too tired and too wasted to cover himself, and as he leant back against the hard, plastered wall, he sensed Cass sit down beside his feet, on the floor.

'Cassie,' he repeated, his heart full of fondness as he reached down to touch her lovely face. She was sweet and kind and generous, and he knew she'd never make any demands of him. When Cass gave pleasure it was to celebrate the moment, and all she asked was the same in return. Tenderness, fun and orgasms – it was as simple and as elegant as that.

'Yes?' she answered, looking up at him, her eyes stormy-dark with languor, and the last of his semen on her lips.

'You're an angel,' he said simply, stroking her cheek, then smoothing his essence from her mouth.

'Fallen one, I think,' Cass grinned.

'Would it upset you if I told you I was still thinking of Dani?'

Why the hell did I say that? he thought as soon as he'd said it. How could I be so hurtful, so crass?

'It'd surprise me if you said you weren't,' she commented lightly, her smile untroubled. 'I was thinking about her while I was sucking you.' Her long pink tongue did another slow circuit of her lips.

'Minx!' he said softly, tousling the thick fluffy strands of her dreadlocks and making her loosely coiled coiffeur deconstruct, 'And what exactly are you doing here anyway? Apart from waylaying hapless dog's-bodies in the course of their chores, then draining their poor bodies dry?'

'Oh, I forgot,' she said guilelessly as she rose to her feet and re-wound her hair as she did so. 'Lois sent me to fetch you . . . She's squawking up a storm 'cos Dani's disappeared and *she's* stuck on the desk doing some work for a change.' Looking Mitch straight in the eye, she smoothed her smock down over her long, tawny thighs, and finally hid her pubis from his gaze.

'You might have told me that,' he said, feigning irritation as he too covered up himself. Slowly, almost meticulously, he replaced his penis in his shorts, then zipped and buttoned his trousers. As he rose to his feet, he noted ruefully that there was a long dark stain on his thigh, where Cass had brought her body to its pleasure.

'I got distracted, Mitch,' she replied, eyeing what she'd done to him, then spinning pertly on her heel and sashaying away across the storeroom. At the door, she paused, and shot him a look. One of her strange sideways glances that disquieted whomsoever they settled on, and reminded them firmly of her origins. 'But not *too* distracted,' she added softly, her voice like mystery and midnight, and her eyes full of Romany wisdom.

As she disappeared, Mitch shuddered to his marrow, and wondered how deeply her special vision had pierced . . .

Cass smiled and listened to the footsteps behind her. She loved it when she put a man off-balance, especially one as gorgeous as Mitch. There was the finest of fine lines to skirt up against, and just now she'd stopped short when she'd reached it. The time to break through wasn't yet . . .

'Where the hell have you two been?' demanded Lois as they returned to Reception, her cool face

162

hot with anger. 'It's bad enough having Daniella disappear, without the rest of the staff going AWOL too!'

Cass remained meek and quiet, armoured by memories of yesterday. Lois was powerless against her, just a cipher now their bodies had touched. Being seen helpless and naked in orgasm had torn down the blonde woman's barriers, and any authority that remained to her was nominal. Cass was polite, and obedient, but her sly secret knowledge made her smile.

'Cassandra, I wonder if you'd take more towels up to Room 6, please?' asked Lois cautiously, as if she were waiting for some show of defiance. 'I don't know what on earth they're doing with them . . . They had the usual batch of fresh ones this morning.'

'You got it!' Cass replied immediately, enjoying the surprise on the other woman's face. There was something to be said for keeping *all* her lovers off-balance, she thought cheerfully, as she left the tense atmosphere of Reception en route to the linen store for towels.

Things were getting very interesting here at 'Hotel Aphrodisia', Cass reflected, stepping into the airing cupboard and taking a deep breath of its fresh-washed fragrance. After her years as a traveller, enduring less than hygienic conditions, she took a voluptuous delight in every single thing to do with washing. Newly-laundered linen; the smells of pine and perfume and soap; the experience of bathing itself. There was nothing Cass liked better than to sink into a deep, hot tub piled high with a huge float of bubbles. She'd lather and rinse, and lather and rinse, and derive a profound, deeply sexual pleasure from knowing her skin was squeaky clean.

Dammit, Cass, you got distracted again! she chastised, lifting her face from a deep stack of towels. Just the way you did with old Mitch.

Now that had been a pleasant interlude, she decided as she divided the pile of towels and selected several to take to Room 6. Very pleasant indeed. Licking her lips to recall his salty flavour, she wondered if she ought to feel guilty.

Her instincts – which were generally right – told her it was Dani whom Mitch really wanted. And vice-versa. It was naughty of her, she supposed, to poach either one of them off the other – but they were both so deliciously sexy. And Dani had been – and maybe still was – ensconced with Jamie Rivera. Poor Mitch needed recompense for *that*, it was only fair. And it was better he get it with someone who had Dani's best interests at heart, and not a prissy bitch like Pandora the writer.

Yes, everything was certainly coming to the boil nicely, Cassie observed as she made her way along the corridor, her arms full of fluffy white towelling.

Outside the door of Room 6, she paused to consider the man beyond it.

Perry McFadden, affluent businessman. Very nice if you liked that sort of thing – the prosperous beautifully-preserved older type. Which Cass admitted she did . . . It was a shame about his Barbie-doll secretary though. She was bound to be hanging around somewhere, and Cass would have preferred a clear shot. What had happened with Mitch in the storeroom had simply been a tasty little appetiser and now she was ready for a meal.

Her knock wasn't answered, so feeling slightly let down, she opened the room with her pass-key.

164

The sense of disappointment didn't last long however, not even thirty seconds, because the room hadn't been empty for long, and its occupants had clearly left in a rush.

It *had* to have been a rush, because no one in their right mind would have left out such things as *this*.

12   A Game In Black Vinyl

'OH BOY,' MURMURED Cass, dropping her forgotten towels on a chair, 'What the devil has been going on here?' With her eyes wide open and her libido stirring, she picked up an item from the bed.

Cass had never been over-fond of underwear, even now, when she'd abandoned her life on the road. She preferred her body to feel free and untrammelled, without the strictures of bras and pants and all the other fripperies that passed as feminine 'lingerie'. The garment she picked up from the bed, however, made her wonder about what she'd been missing.

Not that it was anything like the undies most women wore . . .

Perry McFadden was obviously a fetishist, and had been trying to make 'Barbie' one too. Cass picked up a shiny black PVC basque from her bed and held it assessingly against herself, intrigued by its squeaky, super-glossiness and the way the material clung stickily to her fingers. Turning the thing this way and that, she saw that it fastened at the back with a lacing of criss-crossed silk cords, and at the front with tiny hooks and eyes. It was very short, too, and she guessed it would probably come no further down than her belly button; while at the top, the bra-cups were just crescent-shaped shelves that would support the naked bosom to perfection, yet hide nothing from the beholder's lustful eye.

A cheaper version of the same basque would have been extraordinarily sleazy, but this one was craftsman-finished and obviously expensive. The stitching and construction was meticulous, and every hem and edge was trimmed with a micro-fine line of black lace that had the unmistakable sheen of pure silk. Cass could well imagine how a woman who wore something so stunning might be worshipped and wanted, her barely-clad body adored. Then again, she thought wryly, picking up several small arrangements of straps and buckles – in the same gleaming stuff as the basque – the wearer could just as easily be a man's victim. A tender, tightly-trussed delicacy to satisfy the most warped of desires.

'Oh God,' whispered Cass. The second image was far more exciting. She pictured herself bound into the sheeny-black corset, her hands and her ankles cruelly strapped. The bed was strewn with a variety of other esoteric knickknacks, and before she could stop it, or control it, her mind played with some of these too.

There was a large – impossibly large – flesh-coloured vibrator, and this would be pushed deep inside her womanhood while unseen hands governed its speed.

Next to the dildo were several sets of tiny silver clamps. What were they for? she wondered, picking one up and testing its springiness. An ear? A nipple? Somewhere even more intimate? Shuddering with a strange anticipation, she dropped the wicked thing back on the bed.

Deary me, he's really into this in a big way, she thought, as she examined more and ever stranger paraphernalia. Gags, handcuffs, a small, rounded bulbous object that made her clench the muscles of her bottom as she handled it. What a pity McFadden had brought 'Barbie' with him, Cass reflected as she retrieved the basque from the heap and held it to her for a second appraisal.

I could play these games, she observed, looking at her body and the corset in the mirror. I'd be a natural . . . I bet I could teach *him* a thing or two. On impulse, she dropped the basque on a chair and started undoing her overall, fumbling with the buttons in her haste.

The shiny, reptilian black fabric looked stunning against the honey of her skin, and for a moment Cass considered wriggling quickly into it. It would only take a second or two to fasten the laces, although the hooks and eyes were more tricky . . .

But you're all sweaty, Cass, she told herself. You've been cleaning all day, and you had sex less than an hour ago . . . She touched the delicate satin lining of the basque, then shuddered at the thought of her grubby, grungy body inside it.

I could always take a bath though . . .

As soon as she thought it, she knew it was fatal. She imagined the luxurious tub in the next room, and could almost smell the scented bath essence that was provided free of charge for the guests. There were even several different ones to choose from: pine or lemon based for the men, and rose or gardenia for the women . . .

You're going to do it, aren't you, Jenkins? she thought despairingly. You're going to do it . . . and you know it's only a matter of time before you get caught.

A minute later she was standing by the deep, glistening porcelain bathtub – the one she herself had polished earlier – and waiting for it to fill up with water. This was Cass's secret vice at the Bouvier Manor, her clandestine thumbed-nose to Richard, Lois and all the glamorous, well-heeled guests.

'Nice one, Cass,' she murmured as she sank down into the silky-textured water. There was something so heavenly about a stolen bath, a decadence that aroused her intensely. Beneath the surface of the gently rocking bubbles, her hand moved purposefully to her sex. 'Mmmm, another nice one,' she purred, encountering a different kind of silkiness, the slippy moisture of desire.

Lolling dreamily in flower-scented suds, Cass let her mind float too. She thought of her pleasure with Mitch, her short, rather piquant encounter with Lois, and the tenderness she'd finally shared with Dani. Scooping up water in her palm, she let it trickle down over her breasts where their upper slopes breached the thick, fragrant foam. She smiled, thinking of all the things Dani had said about the water. How she'd blamed it for her obsession with sex.

'I don't know, Dani my love,' she murmured pensively. 'I really and truly don't know . . .' There were certain unusual mineral elements in the water, slight traces that Cass – with her extensive knowledge of wells and natural springs – could identify by taste. But there were no classic aphrodisiac ingredients in there, no gypsy magic such as Cass had used before.

Did it affect the guests? she wondered, soaping her shoulders, her chest and her arms one-handed, while below she still touched her swollen folds. Something had definitely pumped up Perry McFadden's sex-drive, she decided, and sent it down paths that were very strange indeed.

As she glanced idly around the bathroom, she noticed something else that was strange. There was nothing of 'Barbie's' in the room; no hairspray, no drying tights, no make-up. Had Perry's PA done a bunk? she wondered. Were the basque and the dildo too much?

As Cass considered this possibility, a noise in the bedroom beyond almost made her panic and submerge. She knew she should have expected to be caught – the odds had predicted it long ago – but it was still one almighty shock. Holding herself perfectly motionless in the water, she listened for voices, but heard none. There were only the faint sounds of movement, and the clink of a bottle against a glass.

The sense of tension was peculiarly titillating. Cass felt deliciously comfortable in the water, and yet she was in jeopardy. She was in an environment of total relaxation, yet every nerve in her body was jumping . . .

Come on in, you bastard! she called out silently, but the only answer she got was the glass again. Twice. Come on, you drunken sot! she willed him furiously, wondering what was causing such a single-minded consumption of booze.

Losing her patience, and a little of her courage, she rose gracefully out of the water – just at the very instant the bathroom door opened.

Perry McFadden's face was a picture. It was clear that the last thing he'd expected was a naked water nymph in his bathroom, and judging from the strained look about his eyes, his slightly dishevelled appearance, and the whisky filled tumbler in his hand, he didn't seem to be expecting *any* kind of female at all. Cass's suspicion he'd been deserted gained substance.

The tall businessman was an engaging-looking man, even if at present he appeared a bit frayed around the edges. As Cass eyed him warily – whilst framing her excuses – he pushed a hand through his thick, slightly silvered hair and regarded her in total amazement. Neither of them spoke, but as Cass stepped out of the tub and dripped profusely on the bathmat, Perry took a long, deep pull of his drink.

'I . . .' Cass began, then faltered when he drained his glass, reached for a towel, then politely held it out to her. She was just about to take it from him, when suddenly he seemed to change his mind, and instead of just passing the bathsheet to her, he moved forward, unfolded it in a single elegant flick, and draped it around her naked shoulders.

'Well, this is an unexpected pleasure,' he said, his voice a little blurred from the whisky. 'I'm Perry McFadden . . . Pleased to meet you.'

Folding her towel around her, Cass turned slightly and hid her smile of triumph. She couldn't have made a better impact on Perry McFadden if she'd tried. His face bore a look of thunderstruck surprise mixed with a genuine "there is a God" happiness, as if she – in all her naked glory – were the answer to his most heartfelt prayers.

'Pleased to meet you too,' Cass replied cheerfully. 'And I'm Cassandra Jenkins.' She held out her slender, gilded hand.

'Well, I'm either drunk or I'm dreaming . . .' He looked quizzically at his empty glass. 'My girlfriend walks out on me calling me a pervert because I want to play a few games . . . and less

171

than twenty minutes later I find a beautiful, naked woman in my bathroom. I must've done something right somewhere.' Still slightly bemused he put his tumbler on the vanity unit, then took Cass's hand and raised it courteously to his lips.

'I'm only your chambermaid, I'm afraid,' Cass pointed out, adjusting the towel to show her breasts to advantage.

'There's no "only" about it from where I'm standing,' said Perry with a grin, his eyes – which were a deep smoky grey – clearing as he seemed to shake off the effects of the whisky. 'I'd say you were a gift from heaven . . . but what on earth were you doing in my bath?'

Cass felt the pit of her stomach go as soft as melted honey. She'd always had a thing about distinguished older men who kept their bodies in the peak of condition, and Perry McFadden filled all these criteria. She estimated him to be in his early fifties, but he was still lithe and slim and he exuded a palpable sexiness in his faded, tight-fitting blue jeans. His casual white shirt was unbuttoned at the neck, and showed a throat that looked both strong and vulnerable, as well as a little wiry chest hair that peeked out of the deepest part of the vee. There was an appealing outdoors-man ruggedness about his face, and a touch of mischief around his mouth and his eyes. He was a man with a sense of adventure, despite his years and his sharp business lifestyle, and Cass decided that 'Barbie' was an idiot.

She also decided to be honest. 'It's a little quirk of mine, you might say. A sort of fetish . . . I get turned on by baths and bathing, and whenever I see a tub, I get this overpowering urge to get into it and wallow in bubbles.'

172

'That's interesting,' observed Perry, moving in tentatively behind Cass, and touching her back with the lightest of pressures, 'A fetish, you say . . .' He shot her a glance, his dark eyes twinkling. 'And did wallowing in *my* bath turn you on?'

'A little,' lied Cass, as they passed through into the bedroom. She eyed the objects still spread out on the bed. 'But not nearly as much as all that stuff. Were you planning an orgy or something?'

Perry looked glum for a moment. 'I brought someone away with me for a few days of fun . . .' His fine mouth narrowed – which was a shame, Cass thought. 'I thought we were on the same wavelength, but it turned out we weren't . . .'

'She's a fool,' said Cass softly, evading Perry's hand, and walking towards the bed. 'This is amazing!' She picked up the basque, and as she did so, let her towel drop away. Turning, she held the glassy black basque against her, and watched Perry's eyes blaze hot with naked lust.

'It's beautiful,' she continued, twisting this way and that as if posing in front of a mirror. 'I could wear something like this . . .'

'Could you?' The hope was almost tangible in his voice.

'Absolutely,' she replied, 'Would you like me to put it on now? I'd need some help . . .' She ran her fingers down the intricate lacing.

'I'd be glad to help you,' Perry said, moving quickly towards her, and taking her in his arms with the basque squashed in between their bodies. Looking down into her eyes, he pushed his hardened crotch lightly against her belly. 'We could have a little fun together, Cassandra . . . If you like? And I could forget about the "fools" of this world . . .'

173

It was a slice of delicate emotional blackmail, thought Cass as his mouth came down hungrily on hers, but it was something she'd always been a sucker for. This virile and – she sensed – rather good-hearted man definitely deserved *something* in the way of cheering up.

The basque stuck to her breasts as they kissed, its bones digging into her midriff while Perry crushed her tightly against him and foraged in her mouth with his tongue. Cass could feel her vulva growing heavy, and her entire body opening like a flower. It would be exciting to confine these sensations in the corset, she realised, and to sample the perversity of constriction instead of her usual mellower pleasures. Greedy to move forward, she freed herself easily from the kiss and held out the basque towards Perry.

Her new friend smiled, a slow, almost dreamy smile as if anticipating the voluptuousness ahead. With a deftness that suggested this wasn't the first time he'd handled such garments, he loosened off the lacings, then lifted the basque above her head and indicated she streamline herself into it.

Cass felt a thrill just from the thing sliding slowly down her body. The sleek silk lining seemed to coast along her skin like a caress in itself, and she got even more little shocks of stimulation when Perry's fingers repeatedly touched her. With an excitingly discriminating accuracy, he settled the corset loosely around her waist, then lifted her hands so she could hold it in place to be tightened.

As she'd suspected, the basque left her belly, her sex and her bottom quite bare, and though the cups would have covered a small fraction of her breasts, Perry arranged her so they were completely exposed. His touch on her now-tender globes was quite rough, as if he were still a little nervous, and as he propped each rounded breast on its narrow vinyl platform, he squeezed her nipples and pinched them very gently.

It was a treatment that drove Cass frantic. The tiny pain made her swollen vulva ripple, and her hips waft wildly to and fro.

'Oh God, you're a sexy woman, Cassandra,' he hissed in her ear, still squeezing with one hand while with the other he let down her hair.

Cass's own fingers were tingling. They seemed filled with a peculiar electricity, a mad urge to stroke and pleasure her sex. She wanted desperately to masturbate, but decided to wait for Perry's permission. She sensed it was a part of his game, the reason he'd wrapped her up in plastic, like a love-doll adorned for his pleasure.

'Turn round, Cassie,' he said suddenly, and she smiled inside at his instinctive use of her pet name. 'Lean forward, spread your legs, and brace yourself against the bed. I'm going to lace you up.'

Just the words made Cass sweat and shake, and as she obeyed she felt a tiny plume of bliss. Acutely aware of her stance, she almost came from her own sense of exposure. Her defenceless-ness . . . She was bent at the waist, with her stiff arms holding her up from the bed and her rear thrust backwards towards Perry. Without a word, and as if taking the gift that she offered, he squeezed and fondled her bottom-cheeks in just the same way he'd handled her breasts. Taking a lobe in each hand, he moved it around strongly, then let her smooth flesh bounce as he released it.

'Lovely,' he murmured after about a minute of

this treatment, then turned his attention to the laces. Adjusting the tension from the small of her back to the middle of her ribcage, he took hold of them and started to pull.

The effect began almost immediately. Cass felt her internal organs being compressed and forced downwards and pressing inexorably on her sex from within. Her vulva bulged out like an over-ripe fruit, the pressure so intense it was almost exquisite.

When Cass was sure that the corset was as tight as it could possibly be, Perry let her gather herself for a moment, and then began another round of pulling. She felt her breath start to shorten, and her belly harden like the skin of a drum. Her sex was so full and wet, it felt ready to explode, and she was convinced that any second she'd climax.

When Perry was finally satisfied with the laces, he pushed her forward on to the bed and encouraged her to kneel up on all fours.

'Gorgeous,' he whispered, running his hands over her vinyl-bound body. Cass whimpered as his fingertips traversed her hot skin; every inch of her seemed doubly, no trebly sensitised, and even the areas that were covered felt his touch.

He was examining her, she realised, testing the texture and response of her flesh. Seeing how warm she was; how wet; how sweaty and slick with her nectar. His hands moved indiscriminately over both sexual zones and others ones; one moment dipping deeply and uninhibitedly beneath her legs, the next, shaping lovingly around the arch of her foot.

'Move about a bit,' he instructed, his voice gruff with arousal. 'Waggle your hips for me, that's it . . . Spread your legs, Cassie . . . exhibit yourself.'

Exhibit yourself? Even the words made her

giddy . . . Going forward on her elbows, Cass swayed her hips slowly from side to side, and imagined what Perry would be seeing. Her rounded bottom, framed by the corset and its eding of lace, and the dark fruity chasm of her sex. The idea of it made Cass quiver, and when two fingers pushed inside her, she squealed.

'Do you like that?' he whispered, leaning over her, his breath lightly scented with whisky. 'You know you want it . . . You're so wet. So naked and open and ready . . .'

Cass smiled at how right he was. Flexing her spine, she pushed herself back on to his hand and gripped his fingers with the muscles of her sex.

'She-cat . . . Horny little devil,' he muttered, rubbing his face in the fluffy softness of her hair and nibbling at her ear as he pumped her.

Groaning, Cass fell forward against the bed-spread and felt orgasm rampage through her loins. It was quick, hard and shocking, and as her sex pulsed around Perry's fingers, she bit hard on the thick chenille cover.

'So beautiful . . .' hissed Perry, waggling his fingers teasingly inside her and making her whimper and drool.

But just as she was soaring on their motion, the pleasuring fingers were withdrawn. 'That's enough for now,' said Perry, his voice playfully severe. 'You've been a naughty girl . . . You shouldn't be enjoying yourself so much.'

Try and stop me, thought Cass defiantly, her vulva still fluttering as Perry rolled her over on to her back. She lay inert as he arranged her body, pushing her thighs apart, and making her stretch her arms out over the bed above her head. Her sex was completely open and unguarded, and her breasts were lifted and displayed for inspection.

She was spread like a star on her gentle captor's bed, every part of her available to his touch.

Cass felt her whole body screaming silently for attention, yet still playing, Perry ignored her. Turning away, he prepared himself another drink, picked up and studied various items from the bed, and then eventually seemed to select several, obviously to use in the game.

As she watched and listened, Cass couldn't help squirming, her own plight beginning to plague her. Her arousal was extreme now, as if a ball of tension was swelling in her belly and bearing down on a thousand strung-out nerve-ends, each one of them connected to her clitoris. She imagined touching herself, then rubbing herself furiously. The orgasm would be massive and noisy, and she wondered if Perry would be cross if his wishes were pre-empted.

Or mock-cross, she thought slyly, not sure whether she wanted to be punished for her naughtiness, or played with, or both. Moving uneasily amongst the disorder of the bed, she wondered if she dare clutch her vulva, to ease the gnawing ache that assailed it.

'Wicked girl,' said Perry sternly as Cass finally pressed her fingers to her pussy. 'No pleasure for you until I say so.'

'But I need it,' pleaded Cass, injecting a whining, little-girl note into her voice, and feeling pleased when Perry's eyes brightened. So that *was* what he liked, eh?

'You'll have to wait, my sweet,' he said, moving closer and looking down at her. 'We haven't played our games yet, have we?' He reached down and stroked her cheek with an extra-ordinary tenderness, a light, almost loving touch which was strangely unnerving.

'No . . . Oh no . . .' moaned Cass, scissoring her legs slowly, her body stirred by both frustration and the unexpectedness of Perry's affection. She'd travelled light all her life, physically and emotionally, and real contact, and real caring, were something rare and wonderfully precious. She suddenly realised she'd do anything for this man, and play any game, no matter how dangerous and deviant.

Perry touched her again, on her brow this time, and her vulva fluttered wildly, silently pleading that he touch her there too.

'You're so lovely . . . So responsive,' he murmured, his expression intensely absorbed. Looking up from her well of desire, Cass could see a strange near-rapture on his face, a profound inward focusedness. As if this game, or whatever it was they were going to share, meant something far more than just sex to him, that it was mystic. A communion. A rite . . .

As Perry moved around the room, making his preparations, Cass let her mind drift backwards in time. She thought of her days on the road, and Robbo, a wild, half Spanish youth who'd been sexually sophisticated to a degree that was far beyond his years. They'd tried everything, and then some, but *their* games had always had meaning too.

She remembered a day when he'd tied her to a seat in his van, naked from the waist down, then driven several hundred miles in one haul. He'd stopped now and again, untied her and let her walk about, then allowed her to relieve herself under his close surveillance. Each time they'd returned to the van, he'd stimulated her gently but thoroughly to the very point at which she was sobbing for an orgasm, then bound her again and

179

carried on with the journey. Cass had been unable to do anything to help herself with her hands strapped tightly at her sides.

After many long hours, when she'd been almost beside herself, he'd pulled the van off the road and driven along a track to a small secluded clearing. Cass had groaned, and almost fainted with longing when he'd helped her get out of the van, then set her down on her feet on the turf. Once more he'd allowed her to empty her bladder, but held her hands so she couldn't touch her pussy. Even so she'd almost come when he'd blotted her with a tissue.

When they'd reached a young narrow-trunked tree, he'd stripped her completely, then bound her to the tree with leather belts: her bare back pressed tight against the bark, her thighs wide apart and her ankles flexed to curve around the trunk.

Then, ignoring her desperate cries that he take her, and her writhings and struggles against the tree, he'd begun arousing her all over again. He'd started by stroking everywhere on her body but her sex with the sweetest and gentlest of caresses. He'd covered her breasts, her arms, and her neck with featherlight kisses, while his fingertips had roamed teasingly across her belly.

When he'd finally touched her clitoris, she'd screamed, climaxed violently, and her juices had trickled down her legs. While she was still throbbing, and still lost in pleasure, he'd entered her and called her his 'goddess' . . .

Despite her position of subservience, Cass felt almost divine right now. She was Perry McFadden's sexual totem, the focus of his passion and lust. He wanted her, she knew that, but despite that her own desire was greater. It felt like an esoteric love-toy inside her; a giant ball of pressurised heat that seemed to caress her aching clitoris from within.

Perry's final refinements were almost unnecessary, but as a connoisseur of the kinky, she enjoyed them. From the bed, he picked up an item she'd admired earlier – a luxurious, velvet commedia dell'arte blindfold – and placed it reverently across her eyes. Its soft, satin lining was cool against her face, and behind it she was left in total darkness. Excitingly sightless now, she felt him bind her hands gently to the bed-head, then do the same – using what felt like woven silk cords – to her ankles, at the foot-board.

'No! Oh no!' she protested when she heard him step back again, as if to leave her. Every nerve-end in her body was tingling, every square inch of her skin, uncovered, or covered by the corset, was crying out for some kind of stimulation.

'Now,' said Perry, his voice as velvety as the beautiful black mask, 'we're going to play a game of deduction and judgement. I'm going to touch you, in a variety of ways . . . and you have to decide what I'm using on you, then choose how you want me to make you climax.'

The first contact was light, ephemeral, as insubstantial as if he were simply breathing on her. The most delicate of sensations slid like mist over her neck and her shoulders, then passed down across the basque to her hip. Floating, almost aggravating, it flicked up and down the insides of her thighs, up and down, barely discernible, yet goading her like fire. Her vulva pouting and running, Cass arched up in her bonds to try and get more of it, yet as she did so,

Perry lifted the torment away . . .

'So, little Cassie, what was that?' he enquired, his voice soft and impish against her ear.

Panting, hardly able to speak, Cass gasped out the answer. The easy answer, because she'd seen this particular object earlier, amongst the toys on the bed, and *not* amongst the others of its kind, which stood in the vase that adorned the empty fireplace.

'A feather . . . A peacock feather from the fireplace . . .'

'Correct!' said Perry, drawing the soft, tickling fronds against her pubis, then laughing indulgently when she groaned with thwarted lust. 'Clever girl,' he went on pensively, then for several long moments there was near silence, except for the small sounds of him sipping his whisky.

What now? she thought deliriously. She couldn't endure much more and stay sane. Every part of her vulva was so sensitised it almost pained her, and her clitoris felt ten times its normal size.

The next item was easy too. Coldness trickled over the planes of her belly, then pooled like liquid bliss on the overheated creases of her groin. She squealed in shock though, when something even colder, yet softened and running, was slipped deftly into the eye of her navel. Working desperately with her stomach muscles, she tried to flip the chilly thing toward her sex, to either cool her down or finally make her climax, but stubbornly, it just slithered in a circle, and sent cold dribbles between her legs to taunt her.

'And that, my sweet?' enquired Perry.

'An ice-cube . . . In my navel . . . From your whisky,' she whispered.

'Clever girl!' he cried, and she felt his fingertips

182

stirring at the tiny chunk of ice and making streams of water ooze deliciously over her belly. As one trickle seeped slowly between her labia, she yelped at the precursive, almost crystalline pulsation.

She had to wait much longer for the next, and she suspected, the last item, and it was obvious Perry knew she was almost coming.

The sounds of preparation were small and totally indecipherable, and when Perry very carefully parted her labia, she sobbed loudly with delight and relief. Then, within seconds, she felt something being smeared on her, and almost immediately she was orgasming ferociously from the feel of it, whilst not having any inkling in the slightest what it was. As her body throbbed and jumped, and she saw a rainbow of colour in the darkness, she felt Perry pack her shivering sex with the substance.

For a while, Cass couldn't really have said whether she was conscious . . . or drifting in some bizarre, hyperspatial limbo where Perry kept turning into Robbo, then mutating back into simply being himself. He was massaging something slippery and pulpy into the most sensitive part of her, and its strange, slooshy, faintly lumpy texture only enhanced the sublimeness of the fingering.

Lost on a plateau of ecstatic perceptions, Cass suddenly tuned into another of her senses. Not touch this time, but smell; and as she sniffed, and her nostrils filled with a familiar and mouth-watering fragrance, she suddenly *knew* what it was between her legs. It was something she'd tasted just this morning, illicitly, while she'd been about her duties in this very same room.

'What's this then?' asked Perry, and Cass could

183

hear the smile in his voice, as he scooped some of the sweet-smelling goop from between her sex-lips and presumably popped it rudely in his mouth.

'Nectarine,' she whispered, 'I put some in your fruitbowl this morning . . . They're delicious, but they're over-ripe. I know 'cos I pinched one and ate it.'

'Sod nectarines!' said Perry almost violently, and in the next instant his mouth was on her sex, lapping and licking at her fruit-daubed membranes and sucking voraciously at the bud of her clitoris. 'You're the one that's delicious,' he muttered, lifting his face for just a second, then plunging back down into the messy feast.

Crying out in a long continuous climax, Cass had neither voice nor will to argue. She could only surrender to the mastery of his tongue.

When the tumult was finally over, she just lay there glowing in her bonds, while Perry kissed his way upwards from her juice-anointed sex. Traversing her wet belly, and the sleek black containment of the corset, he eventually found her throat, face, and mouth.

'You lost the game,' he whispered, nibbling her lower lip, then letting her taste both the nectarine and herself. 'You came before I'd finished my three items.'

'Is there a forfeit?' Cass enquired, smiling dreamily into the blackness behind her mask.

'Yes,' he said, his voice gruff as he levered himself over her, and she discovered that some of the small sounds she'd heard had been him taking his clothes off. 'And I'm afraid you have to pay it right now . . .'

Cass smiled again, raising her head to find his lips with her own.

Perry had posed his little challenge, she thought contentedly, and was now entitled to his forfeit. But as a stiff cock brushed and bounced against her thigh, and nimble fingers reached quickly down to guide it, she was fully aware of who'd *really* won the game . . .

13 The Storm before the Calm before the Storm

DANI SLEPT BADLY that night.

She should have slept well after her satisfying afternoon with the delightful, obedient, and very accomplished Jamie Rivera, but the atmosphere back in Reception afterwards had almost erased her sexy romp from her mind.

She'd expected trouble, and a telling off for staying in Jamie's room so long, but it was the very lack of any of these that had unnerved her. The absence of Mitch and Cass had bothered her too. Her co-conspirators were nowhere to be seen, leaving a somewhat subdued Lois to oversee the desk.

The Assistant Manageress had seemed nervous and preoccupied, so much so that she hadn't even commented on Dani's long absence; and though they'd never been the best of friends, Dani couldn't help feeling concerned about Lois. The blonde woman's face had been paler than usual, with the tension of deep worry about her mouth. In a person who was normally unassailable these small signs of weakness were scary.

186

'Is anything wrong?' Dani had asked, and the answer was still plaguing her now, almost twelve hours later, in the still, moody half-light of dawn.

There'd been a phone-call, Lois had said. From the head office of MJK . . . The managing director – 'MJK' himself, or the 'boss' as they'd called him – would be taking over tomorrow, with his team . . . and then, probably, all hell would break loose!

And I'm no nearer to knowing who the 'boss' is, thought Dani glumly, turning over – for the hundredth time – in her bed. It'd been an unseasonably cool night and she was snuggled up in an unflattering old nightie for comfort. The winceyette kept her body warm and cosy – but she had hoped for another source of heat.

She'd half expected, and devoutly wished, that Cass would come to her, and had looked forward to some playful, soothing pleasure to distract her mind from the imminent disaster.

But Cass had never turned up, and Dani had the sneakiest feeling that the gypsy girl hadn't even spent the night in her own room either.

Still, Cass was a free agent in every sense of the word, and the last person Dani could make claims on. The same thing could also be said of Mitch, another 'someone' she'd half expected to turn up.

Dani had a nasty feeling that she *knew* why Mitch hadn't come. Regardless of what he'd said this afternoon, she sensed he was profoundly jealous over the time she'd spent with Jamie. Even though he himself was the one who'd encouraged her to check out the delectable tennis star.

And they say women are the contrary ones! she thought, turning over in bed, exasperated.

After perhaps another hundred of such turns, surprisingly Dani fell asleep. She didn't recall the moment when she slipped away, but suddenly she was woken by a tiny, almost unaudible creak. The sound of her bedroom door being pushed open.

'Who is it?' she called as she sat up, although a firefly glint in the half-light had already identified the intruder.

'Just me,' said Mitch quietly, moving closer, his eyes still invisible behind his glasses.

Dani had wanted this, but now she'd got it she was nervous. There were bound to be questions about Jamie, and she didn't think Mitch would like the answers – or the method she'd employed to obtain them.

'What do you want, Mitch?' she asked warily, pulling the blankets up virginally to her chin.

'I thought we'd better have a talk,' he replied. His voice sounded extremely odd, and for a moment Dani couldn't work out why. Then she realised his teeth were chattering, and that no matter how tough he liked to think he was, the icy dawn air was too cold for him.

'At five o'clock in the morning?' she demanded, taking a calculated guess at the time.

'I couldn't sleep . . . I needed to compare notes.' He was obviously getting chillier and chillier by the second, because he was chafing his bare arms with his hands.

'Well, *I* could sleep . . . Just. But now I can't. Really Mitch, you are the limit. Couldn't it at least have waited till breakfast?'

'No, it couldn't,' he replied, his suddenly steely voice making Dani start to shiver beneath her covers.

There was a long peculiar silence, and Dani was just about to break it, with more protests, when Mitch spoke up again, his tone a little ameliorated this time.

188

'I'm really cold, Dani. I don't suppose I could get in there with you, could I? I won't try anything funny . . . Promise.'

It was a preposterous request, and an outright fib, Dani knew. But after the strange hostility of a moment ago, the thought of his body-warmth was welcome.

'All right, get in,' she said, trying not to sound too encouraging as she held up the covers and moved over.

She'd fully expected Mitch to be naked when he got in beside her – just to plague her – but when their bodies touched, she detected some clothing. Just a pair of thinnish cotton boxer shorts, but at least it was a gesture of propriety.

'What's this?' he asked softly, running his fingers down the sleeve of her nightie. 'I've always pictured you in something silky and slinky and lacy, not a Victorian grandmama's passion killer.' He chuckled mischievously in the darkness, and adjusted his body in the bed.

Dani was amazed at how, for such a tall and substantial man, Mitch commandeered so little of their space. In order not to crowd her, he'd arranged his long, large form so he was lying on his side, and not at any point touching her, although for Dani's part that made little difference. Just his heat was enough to charge her senses.

'Well, you were dead wrong, weren't you,' she observed, her whole body tensed so she didn't roll against him, 'Now, if you'd just get on with it, and tell me what it is you're so desperate to discuss?' As she spoke, another thought occurred. 'And, if you were so keen to "compare notes", where were you at teatime?'

She sensed Mitch's whole body tighten. 'I

'needed to be alone for a while,' he answered, sounding vague. 'You know ... Think things over ...'

Men! she thought again. Always the moody ones ...

'Okay, Greta Garbo,' she said evenly, 'let's get to the point, shall we?'

He moved in the bed again, and this time, brushed lightly against her, his bare thigh touching hers through the nightdress.

'Did you find out anything useful about Jamie Rivera?' he enquired matter-of-factly, as the pressure of his thigh increased a little.

Dani was glad that the light was still poor, because otherwise Mitch would have seen her blushing. What could she tell him? she pondered. There was clear evidence that he was jealous, so whatever she said would either hurt him or annoy him or both.

'Well ... Everything and nothing really,' she evaded.

Mitch remained silent, but the air between them vibrated with his questions.

'I did discover a useful lever we could use against him though ...'

'And what's that?' The thigh pressed just a tiny bit harder, and the body that drove it tilted subtly.

'A certain foible of his ... Something incriminating the press would just love.' She could feel him demanding she explain. 'But it's no use at all to us really, because there's nothing else. He's not the new owner, I'll swear to it!'

'I believe you,' said Mitch quietly, moving yet again. A good deal more of his body was lying against her now: his chest and an arm sneaking across her, both his thighs, and his pelvis with his cock at its centre. Beneath his flimsy boxer shorts

190

his erection was as hard as stone, and Dani could feel it pulsing slightly. His response was in no way unexpected, in fact it had only been a matter of time, but still she quivered finely against it.

'I'm sorry,' he mumbled, as if he'd genuinely not intended to stiffen. 'Don't think badly of me, Dani,' he went on quietly, drawing back a little way from her so they could just see each others faces in the gloom.

In spite of her pre-occupation with his sex jabbing her belly, Dani was taken aback by Mitch's solemnity. His face was oddly serious, his brown eyes dark and grave behind his glasses. There was something more here than a bit of body-rubbing, but *because* of that body-rubbing, her mind couldn't focus on the issue.

'I don't think badly of you, Mitch,' she said, leaning in towards him and closening their contact, 'You're a teasing bastard and an unprincipled sex-fiend, but they aren't neces-sarily *bad* things to be.' She felt his sigh like a zephyr across her face. 'Well, not always . . .'

'I'm glad,' he whispered, accepting the press of her body and manoeuvring it so his hardness met the apex of her thighs and caressed her pubic mound through their clothes.

Dani moaned quietly, almost shocked by her own arousal. She hadn't realised she was so turned on, so sensitised. The blind push of Mitch's cock had almost triggered her. Clumsily, she reached up to touch his face, to encourage or praise or what, she didn't quite know, and her searching hands found the hard frames of his glasses.

'Do you even wear these things in bed?' she asked, laughing.

'Not as a rule,' he answered back, removing the

offending spectacles, and twisting away from her a second to get rid of them.

When he faced her again, fitting his body back against hers, his eyes were brighter without their glass filters. Dani could see strange lights burning in their depths, moods and intensities that were more than desire, more than lust. As he moved in to kiss her, she sensed there was far more to Joseph Mitchell than she'd at first perceived – a million sophisticated complexities beneath the surface – but when their lips met he was just sexy Mitch. Mitch the strong, the randy, the direct. Mitch, whose gorgeous, rampant body was even now begging for entry into hers.

His kiss was deep and luscious, a moist exploration of her mouth that was as erotic as the final penetration. His tongue gently probed her while his hands moved across her covered skin – and both facets of the embrace were strangely measured. Careful. Considerate. Designed to please and not to frighten. Dani could smell a rich, delicious cologne all around them, migrating outwards from warm, clean skin. The scent was intoxicating and seemed to fill up her head like a love-drug. Unconsciously, she ground her hips against him.

'You're lovely,' he whispered, beginning the slow, slow raising of her hem. As he nibbled the sensitive hollows of her throat, she could feel his fingertips making a walking motion on her hip, and bunching up the loose winceyette.

First her ankles were exposed, then her knees, and finally the very tops of her wildly-quaking thighs. She gasped when a large, warm hand enclosed one of her buttocks, the fingers curling neatly in towards her sex. Her vulva was already wet and juicy, and she imagined how it must feel to his touch.

Somewhere in the course of their shufflings, Mitch had slid an arm beneath her body, and with this, he pressed her pelvis against his cock, while his free hand worked its magic on her bottom. Very very delicately, he stroked her labia, her perineum and her anus, his touches as light and soft as the flutter of a dragonfly's wing. The caresses were so insubstantial, so almost inde-finable, that Dani felt an intense desire to scream. To shout out in joyous but maddened frustration for something harder, rougher or more cruel. Anything, but this ethereal, almost ghostly stimulation . . .

But Mitch continued to tantalise, traversing the whole wet area of her sex, whilst avoiding its prime focus, her clitoris. Dani felt wild and frenzied, aware that once again, just as he had beneath the Reception desk, this man held her desperate and bare-bottomed in his thrall.

This time, however, he was allowing her *some* of her own way . . . By wriggling herself against him, she could use his erection to relieve her frustration. Her swollen, softly-furred lips parted naturally around its bulk, and even though it was still tightly contained in thin cotton, his cock was a hard, unyielding fulcrum on which to rock her sorely aching sex. Flexing her legs, and pressing with her toes, she pushed her yearning clitoris against him, then cried out when an instant climax took her – the pleasure infinitely sweet-ened by a finger stroking lightly at her anus.

Groaning, gasping for breath, and coming, Dani felt Mitch let her weight fall backwards. A hand slid between her thighs and rubbed at her still-throbbing clitoris, but she felt his other hand tugging roughly at his shorts. In seconds, she was aware that he was liberated, and before even the slightest fragment of her pleasure had diminished, male flesh was pushing strongly at her gate.

It was as though she'd burst through a discrete and unsuspected membrane, and come out on a whole new level . . . Like a miracle, her orgasm continued, then stepped up a notch, and another and another. Mitch's cock felt huge inside her: a girder, a tree trunk, a mighty projectile moving slowly but surely in her softness. His rhythm was bliss, his heat matchless, and when he kissed her through another massive climax, her consciousness flickered like a flame.

Half-swooning, she clung to his majestically pumping body, instinctively aware that his posture was as classic as his physique. One strong arm was supporting his weight, to keep her slight form from being crushed; while the other curved possessively around her, holding her bottom and bracing her for his thrusts.

'Mitch!' she shouted, her legs kicking crazily, her nails skating across his buttocks and back. 'Mitch! Oh God, I can't stand it!' she howled.

And as her whole belly seemed to melt down to loose atoms, she could have sworn she heard him whisper, 'You must . . .'

When the alarm went, Dani sat up in panic, shouting 'What?'

Had she been dreaming? Had she transferred some particularly steamy fantasy to the sleep-world, and inadvertently chosen Mitch as its star? She liked him . . . Well, far more than liked him . . . But surely not *that* much? In her dream he'd been an idealised god of eroticism, his performance as tender as it was unrelenting. Surely such perfection couldn't happen for real?

But as she moved, a faint but telling twinge said it could. She experienced a tiny trace of soreness as she got up from her bed and started gathering her clothes, but could only smile and deem her battlewound well earned.

So, it had finally happened, she thought, padding to the bathroom, and half hoping she would meet her lover on the landing. They had a lot to talk about. Hitting heights like that didn't happen by accident, so it was obvious they were more than just friends.

Mitch wasn't around, but somehow Dani didn't feel the slightest bit deflated. She sang all the way through her shower; giggling now and again, and challenging the fast-flowing, foam-laced water to make her feel any more sensual than she already felt.

It was only when she reached for her towel that a stray thought – a memory of something Lois had said – popped her warm erotic bubble like a pin.

Oh God, it was *this* morning . . . And the 'boss' and his team arrived today!

14 Enter 'The Boss'

IF THE ATMOSPHERE in Reception had seemed strange yesterday, it had been tranquillity central compared with how the whole hotel felt today . . .

Dani had never once seen Richard up and about so early since she'd started at the Bouvier Manor, and she'd certainly never seen Lois so panicked. The pair of them were like the proverbial cats on hot coals, needlessly sorting out things that didn't matter; because those that *did* matter were beyond being rectified.

There were the usual quota of early rising guests around in Reception too – quite oblivious that the day of reckoning had arrived – and Dani was surprised to see Cass polishing and dusting like fury, with a sleek smile of pure devilment on her face.

'Where the hell did you get to yesterday?' Dani demanded in a moment when she wasn't being ordered about, 'supervised' or questioned. 'I wanted to talk to you about . . . um . . . a certain tennis player. But it just seemed as if you'd disappeared off the face of the earth.'

'I was checking a suspect of my own, Dani-love,' murmured Cass airily, admiring her reflection in some glass she'd just polished. 'Your prime suspect, I might add . . .' She fixed Dani with an impish glance, then winked. 'Mister Perry McFadden, don't you know.'

Dani narrowed her eyes. 'And?'

'Well, he's got secrets all right,' said Cass, licking her born-pink lips.

'Yes, Cass, but are they the ones we're interested in?' Dani felt exasperation simmering. She sensed Cass knew far more than she was telling and that she was deliberately being oblique. Why wouldn't someone give her some answers? She knew she couldn't change anything at this late stage, but stubbornly she still wanted to know the enemy's identity when she met them.

Looking around for someone, or anyone, to stand with her, she felt a burst of exasperation with Mitch too. Weren't they supposed to be in this together? After last night, especially, she'd expected she'd be facing this with him.

What I need is a bit of immoral support, she thought glumly, wondering where on earth her supposed sidekick had got to.

At half past ten, Richard and Lois were still hovering, and Cass was still wielding her trusty Mr Sheen with a fine disregard for economy. Dani had decided there was nothing for it but to treat this as a normal day, and had fallen into her usual efficient routines. She hoped that the guests with their questions didn't notice her slightly strained expression, but as everyone seemed perfectly satisfied with both her answers and her face, there clearly wasn't too much amiss.

Just as she was preparing a bill, three figures appeared ominously in the doorway. Two generic business 'suits' and a smartly dressed super-groomed woman who was obviously some kind of PA.

'May I help you?' Dani asked in what she hoped was a genuine voice. Pasting on a confident smile, she sensed Lois and Richard skulking somewhere behind her like cowards.

'We're here to see the owner of the hotel,' said the sleek woman. 'We work for MJK.'

'Yes, of course,' Dani answered, her heart pounding wildly as she tried to fight her confusion. It was obvious she'd been right, and the owner *was* already here. His – or her – troops had been summoned to the battleground to meet with their supreme commander. 'I'm . . . I'm afraid . . .'

'It's okay,' the PA interrupted smoothly, 'here's the boss now . . .' She nodded towards the wide, central staircase, and Dani hardly dare look up.

The owner of 'Hotel Aphrodisia' was indeed coming down the stairs – resplendent in an Italian designer suit and shoes, glinting here and there with the discreetest hint of gold, and looking the very epitome of sophisticated grace.

Dani was thunderstruck as she stared at the very last person of all she would have suspected. The 'suits' and the PA looked from her to the elegant newcomer standing still at the foot of the steps, and then back again, obviously intrigued by the frozen tableau.

After several eternal seconds, life switched itself back on again.

'Okay, I'll take over now,' said Mitch smoothly, dismissing his minions to their lesser and subordinate roles while Dani looked on open-mouthed. 'Russell, Miss French, may I see you in the Manager's office, please?' he continued, turning his penetrating gold-framed gaze on the wey-faced Manager and his Assistant.

Dani felt numb, stunned to a state of automation. Without being asked, she stepped to a central position behind the desk, and stood ready to be available to the guests.

'Wonderful,' said Mitch quietly, moving towards her. 'I knew I could rely on you.' His expression was still piercing, but somehow softer now; although when he went on his voice retained its briskness, 'If you'd "mind the shop", please, Dani? In your usual superlative style?'

From within a veil of pure ice, Dani summoned a modicum of poise. 'Of course, Mister Mitchell,' she answered evenly, her eyes locking squarely with his.

For the first time since his grand entrance, Mitch looked a little less than masterful. 'It's "Kane" actually,' he offered, 'Mitchell Joseph Kane ... But my friends really do call me "Mitch".'

'I'm sure they do, Mister Kane,' answered Dani smoothly, and if she hadn't been so upset she would have been delighted with her own flash of wit.

'We'll talk later,' said Mitch, his voice quite steady despite his being obviously rattled.

'I'll look forward to it,' Dani replied as he turned and set off for the office.

The numbness thickened around her, but somehow Dani managed to get on with her duties. The first task was to explain to the various guests who were gathered around the desk why the man who had so humbly carried their cases up to their rooms – *and* accepted their tips – was now swanning around in an Armani suit and apparently running the show. Afterwards, Dani had no memory of what she'd told them, but her explanations had seemed to be adequate.

It was only when Cass approached the desk that Dani came out of her trance.

'You knew, didn't you?' she demanded of her friend, reading the gypsy's expression like a book.

'Only since yesterday,' replied Cass, twisting her duster into a tangled orange rag. 'I just sort of twigged it . . . Although for someone who's supposed to have the "sight", I can't figure out why I didn't realise sooner.'

Cass's lovely open face said that this statement was quite true, and Dani felt a tiny fraction better, because she wasn't the only one who'd been blind. Even a Romany seer had been duped by Mitch's tricks . . .

Mitch . . . Goddamn him to hell! As Cass drifted away thoughtfully to get on with her polishing, Dani tried to expunge their mutual traitor from her mind. The brief waking-sleep was gone now, and the full impact of what had happened took her over.

The swine! The bastard! The pig! She'd considered him a friend; she'd made him her lover . . . She'd let him do things to her body that no man had ever done before. And all the time, he'd been lying through his teeth to her. He wasn't good old 'Mitch', her mate, her comrade in adversary. He was Mitchell Joseph Kane, who masqueraded not only as a gofer but also, more subtly, as a mighty corporation. He was a ruthless businessman, exquisitely suave and accomplished. And yet . . . Despite his perfect tailoring, the gold-framed glasses that had replaced his plainer ones, and the slicker grooming of his raven-black hair, he was also the same man who had made love to her.

Swine! Swine! Swine! she raged again inside, and resigned herself to working in *his* hotel for

200

the rest of the morning. What happened then, she still had to decide . . .

It was a morning of comings and goings. Richard and Lois stormed to and fro with documents, ledgers and computer printouts, their faces red and milk pale by turns. Other staff members looked grim as they passed in one direction, then more cheerful as they returned from 'the reckoning'.

At about twelve, even Cass was summoned, and came back looking half flabbergasted and half jubilant. Despite everything, Dani was intrigued.

'You look as if you've dropped a penny and found a tenner,' she observed to the grinning Cass.

'Well, yes . . .' began the gypsy, obviously still mulling over something portentous. 'I've been offered a "prober job" . . . You know, something that's not menial or temporary.'

'What is it?' asked Dani, pleased that her intelligent friend was finally being challenged, but afraid that Cass's wandering spirit might resist it.

'Domestic supervisor. In charge of the cleaning team, plus maintenance and purchasing and everything, and reporting directly to the . . . the manager.'

'Well, I hope to God you're going to take it,' Dani responded pithily, thinking what a sensible innovation it would be – both in the creation of the post, and the choice of the woman to fill it.

'I dunno . . . It all depends . . . There're some other things to be decided before I give him a yea or nay.' Cass's dark eyes were twinkling, and her voice was husky and mysterious.

'Cass?'

'I can't say anything,' the gypsy said defiantly, 'It's all still in the balance.'

'Cassandra Jenkins, you're as devious as *he* is!'

'By "him", I assume you mean the mighty Mitchell?'

'Who else?' hissed Dani caustically.

'He wants to see you,' said Cass, her voice still loaded. 'I'm to cover the desk . . . First time ever . . . That must mean I'm moving up the ladder.'

Before Dani could object, Cass had slid around behind the desk, straightened her smock neatly, and performed her usual alchemy on her hair, changing her loosely-caught bundle of dreads into a surprisingly elegant twist with a few clever flicks of her fingers.

'Well then, go!' she encouraged, smacking Dani surreptitiously on the rump before turning towards an approaching guest with a smile of quite enviable confidence.

Dani had a million questions, and a zillion complaints to voice, but Cass was already charming some poor devil to distraction. With a sigh, Dani made her way to the staff's tiny downstairs cloakroom; not so much to tidy up, because she knew her appearance was as immaculate as ever, but to try and bring order to her thoughts.

It was a difficult task, and not one she managed to complete. As she knocked on the door of the Manager's office, her mind was still a mad, whirling turmoil.

'Come,' called out a voice familiar in timbre but not in its seigniorial intonation. Within was a man in full command mode, not the outrageous, boy-faced scamp who'd plagued her and aroused her for a fortnight.

Mitch rose courteously to his feet as she

entered, and came around to the front of his desk, reaching out as if to take her by the hand. Dani almost danced away from him, her most withering expression on her face. He'd got round her by touching her before, and she was determined it wouldn't happen this time. There was no way she was going to let him bamboozle her, even if the cost was her job.

'I can't say I blame you,' Mitch said, looking sheepish as he pulled up a free chair and sat down close to her, by the front of the desk. 'If I was in your place, I'd hate me too.'

Against her will, Dani sat down too, making an effort to project open, confident body language, and not the hunched up protectionism that she felt.

'What was it you wanted to see me about, Mister Kane?' she enquired coolly.

'Dani, please, it's me, Mitch,' he pleaded, his smooth brow crimping.

'Don't you soft-soap me, you bastard!' she stormed, her ice melting in a flash fire of rage. 'How could you do it? How could you trick me like that? You pretended to be on my side, you pig!' A score of other insults rose to her lips like scalding acid, but her fury was already too much for her. Without conscious thought, and with a strength she hadn't known she possessed, she fetched him a hard, ringing slap across the face, dimly aware she'd hurt her hand in the process.

'You little cat!' Mitch's reaction was primal, and obviously not the reasoned argument he'd planned. Lunging forward, his cheek ablaze, he pulled Dani to her feet and up against him. Before she could draw breath to berate him again, Dani found her mouth firmly muffled, the profanities and protests all stifled by the crushing downforce of his lips. Within seconds his tongue filled her mouth, pushing and ruthlessly possessing, as his strong arms closed tightly against her and ground his groin against the softness of her belly.

Dani was livid. Almost insane with anger. Furious, but with herself just as much as with Mitch. Against her will, her nipples were like iron studs and the niche between her legs like molten lava. She imagined, no, almost *felt* him inside her as he'd been last night. Felt his cock so big and vital as it'd moved in her channel, its rhythm enhanced by his technique and his oh-so-clever subtlety. He was erect already now in his beautiful Italian trousers, so stiff he must surely have been hardening as she'd arrived . . .

'Swine! Arrogant swine!' she spat, then growled around the obstruction in her mouth as she fought with all her might to get free. Twisting and thrashing, she tried desperately to knee him in the groin, but found her leg skilfully trapped between his thighs as her pummelling of his back went unheeded. Her single, tiny triumph was an ill-aimed sideways smack that sent his glasses spinning away towards the floor.

As he began to massage her crotch savagely with his, Dani saw red and bit down on Mitch's snaking tongue.

'Bitch!' he hissed, freeing her mouth, but then kissing her all the harder.

Dani renewed her struggles, but somewhere in the heart of the mêlée, her body suddenly chose to betray her. Hating herself, but powerless to stop what she was doing, she began to squirm her hips and press forward instead of pulling back, her hands sliding deep into Mitch's lustrous hair. Letting her mouth soften, she admitted more of his tongue and then massaged it with hers, loving the sweet, minty taste of his breath.

He's aroused me so easily, she thought, half-dreaming. Set me alight, in spite of myself.

To pull back now would be to cheat her body out of what it wanted, and it wasn't worth it just to win a point. She would have this man, have his sleek, perfectly-groomed flesh and his marvellous, finely-honed muscles. She'd have him, and then discard him, like the double dealing cheat that he was. This would be no affectionate surrender; it was quick, animal satisfaction she wanted, not mellow words to enfeeble her fury.

Sensing a drop in his guard, she pulled away and stared at him venomously.

'Yes, you brute, I want you,' she said in a soft, deadly voice. 'I want use of you, just as you've used me.'

Before Mitch could answer, she spun neatly on her heel, bent over the desk, and hiked up her skirt, knowing full well that what she revealed would inflame him.

'Service me, Mister Kane,' she said crudely. 'It might be the last chance you get.'

'Dani, please,' he groaned, although she could already hear him fumbling with his belt. 'Not like this.'

'Exactly like this,' she commanded, reaching around behind herself, and tugging down her thin lace panties.

Dani bit down on her lip as he entered her. The sensation of being filled was so sublime, so sweet, and even after only one previous occasion, so familiar that she felt like sobbing out aloud with pleasure. Their bodies meshed together so accurately that she was sure there was no finer fit anywhere; and lying prone as she was in this position, she felt Mitch go even deeper than

205

before. She wanted to shout with delight, and encourage him both vociferously and with her eagerly moving body, but to confound him she stayed silent and still. When he reached beneath her belly to caress her, she dashed away his hand, hissing with mock irritation and replacing his fingers with her own.

Just your cock, you horrid monster, she thought, hoping grimly that he understood and felt insulted.

Mitch made no answer, but Dani sensed his acquiescence. He was bent over her now, curving to the shape of her back, his attitude strangely respectful despite his deep-seated possession of her body. Dani felt a curious sense of serenity, an impression of having made her point, and didn't object when he gripped her hip to improve his purchase. His other hand slid forward, along the desk, his fingers searching for hers, pausing, then lacing with them when he sensed he had her permission.

Dani hadn't meant this to happen, but she allowed it, perceiving his touch as a plea for forgiveness. His forging, thrusting penis fell into a rhythm that matched her needs perfectly, but feeling bound to assert herself and her dominance, she chose to complete her own pleasure. With her weight on her forward hand – the one beneath Mitch's – and her thighs jammed against the edge of the desk, she reached down between her legs to find her clitoris.

When she found it, she gnawed her lip again. The sensations were so beautifully intense she could have cried, but she didn't want Mitch to hear a sound. Rubbing herself delicately, she ground her bottom against him, then stiffened rigid as orgasm engulfed her, filling her loins with an icy white flame.

At the pinnacle she could not contain her voice, and her cry rang out loudly around the office. She wondered crazily whether anyone would come in and find them, then relished the idea, her spasms increasing at the thought.

She was still trembling in her climax when Mitch almost collapsed across her back, his supple hips pounding and jerking. She could feel his cock leaping inside her, and then his lips pressing fiercely to the back of her neck as he gasped out a litany of praise.

'Oh Dani! My beautiful beautiful girl,' he babbled. 'Forgive me, my darling love, forgive me.'

There came a moment when her clitoris was too sensitive, and too pleasured, to bear even the slightest touch more. She withdrew her hand, only to have it grabbed, pulled gently backwards and kissed with great passion by Mitch. As he licked and sucked her fingertips, she felt moisture dripping onto the back of her hand, and couldn't believe what her senses were telling her. As Mitch's penis shrank and slid wetly from her body, there were teardrops trickling freely from his eyes. For some reason he was crying like a child . . .

Quietly and very calmly, they drew apart and brought order to their bodies and their clothing. Granting him leave without a word, Dani allowed Mitch to wipe her crotch with his pure silk handkerchief, then watched him stuff the square of soiled fabric in his pocket. She also let him ease her panties back up over her thighs and smooth them carefully into place. Still not saying a word, she sat down in the chair she'd so recently occupied, and accepted the glass of whisky that

207

Mitch poured for her – a generous jigger of some rare triple malt purloined from the cellar by Richard.

'I'm sorry,' said Mitch, resuming his seat too, the one just a foot or two from hers. He was composed again now, and there were no signs of his tears, but his face was extraordinarily serious.

'Again? What are you sorry for now, Mi—' she paused, then made an instant decision, 'Mitch?'

He cracked a faint smile, his eyes brightening visibly behind the glasses she noticed he'd retrieved.

'For everything . . . And for taking advantage just now,' he murmured, looking shamefaced.

Dani took a pull at her drink, appreciating its smoky-smooth flavour. 'What happened just now was what *I* wanted,' she said firmly, looking him levelly in the eye.

'But I didn't deserve to enjoy it so much, did I?' he asked with a soft, sexy laugh.

'No, you didn't.' Dani couldn't help but grin back at him.

'I wanted to tell you, you know,' said Mitch quietly after a short contemplative silence. 'I nearly *did* tell you . . . A hundred times.'

'Then why didn't you?' pressed Dani, crossing her legs, then wishing she hadn't – because the action seemed to tease her sticky sex and trigger an echo of Mitch being inside her. She took another sip of whisky to cover her confusion, but suspected that somehow, Mitch knew what had happened.

'Because you're a good-hearted woman, Dani, and even though I know you've had your differences with Lois and Richard, you'd'd've felt honour bound to warn them of my presence.'

Would she have done? Dani didn't honestly

know. Thinking back over the last few days, she decided that it would have depended just *when* he'd told her.

'And also—' he hesitated, and something in the texture of the silence made Dani study him closely. The killer-light was back in his eyes now, and his face wore its familiar naughty grin. Glancing downwards, she saw the sublimely tailored line of his trousers had a sudden and significant disturbance . . . 'If I'd told you I was Mitchell Joseph Kane and I owned your precious hotel, I might not have been allowed some of the liberties that plain old Mitch could enjoy.'

'I've a feeling you'd still have tried to *take* them,' she answered crisply, 'Mitchell . . . Mitch . . . or whatever it is you call yourself now.'

'Like I said,' he answered, already losing his fleeting air of contrition, 'A man would have to be dead not to try and possess you.'

'Sexist rat!' she countered, surprised by her own note of fondness. After studying the way the whisky swirled around her glass for a moment, she decided it was time – finally – for some straight talk.

'So what happens now?' she enquired, 'I hear you've offered Cass a new job, and I suspect you've sacked Richard and Lois . . . Who's going to manage the Bouvier Manor?'

'Well, I wondered if *you* might consider the job?' replied Mitch, almost airily, only the concentration in his eyes betraying him. 'Alternatively, I could appoint an outsider . . . and you could marry me. Or live with me. Whichever of the two you prefer?'

Dani drank her whisky in one quick swallow, then held out her glass for more, striving desperately to stop her hand shaking. She knew she'd heard him correctly, but even so what he'd said was preposterous. Ridiculous. Unthinkable. Totally mad.

But was it? She sipped from her topped up glass, trying to consider her options dispassionately in the face of Mitch's hope-filled expression.

The first offer was quite viable really. She knew very well she was up to the job, and suspected Mitch knew it too, or he wouldn't have asked her. She loved her dear old 'Hotel Aphrodisia', and being its manager was the position she'd always aspired to . . .

The only problem was the second offer.

'Would you mind if I slept on my decision?' she said finally, when the tension in Mitch's handsome face was as unbearable for her as it obviously was for him.

'No . . . Of course not,' he said, the play of emotion still evident in his eyes. He seemed half-pleased, half scared, and uncharacteristically, in something of a dither.

'But is there any chance that you could sleep on it with *me*?' he blurted out finally, looking extraordinarily young and unsure of himself.

'Of course, Mister Kane,' she answered benignly, putting her glass down and leaning forward, 'But would that be later . . . or now?'

If Mitch answered, the sound was lost beneath the pressure of his lips, and either way, Dani had no doubts what he'd say . . .

I'll take it that's a 'now', she thought happily as he kissed her, and slid his hands beneath the jacket of her suit.

'Have you decided yet?' asked Mitch, a long while later. It wasn't yet night, but they'd both been sleeping, relaxed by long hours of pleasure.

They were in Mitch's room, part of the suite he'd moved into this morning when he'd ceased being a junior desk clerk-come-gofer, and started being the hotel's new owner.

Half-ignoring him, Dani gazed dreamily around their luxurious surroundings and studied the casual accoutrements of his power. The ubiquitous laptop computer stared at them from the desk, designer clothing lay scattered on the floor where he'd dropped it, and his briefcase was spewing documents all across the bedside rug. It was clear that Mitch had genuinely intended to work today – there were profit projections, new staffing structures and God alone knew what else all piled in haphazard heaps all over the place; but the fact they were now totally forgotten brought a smile to Dani's kiss-bruised lips.

It had been like having sex with an entirely different man, she realised now. Different both to the cheeky sidekick of last night, and to the adversary of this morning in the office. With the masks off, Mitch was an assured and accomplished lover whose ever-so-slight vulnerability added a hot spice of deliciousness to everything. Whilst whispering sweet nothings, Dani had suddenly asked him how old he was. When he'd been 'Mitch the dog's-body' she'd unconsciously assumed he'd be her age or thereabouts, but a business tycoon worth millions could hardly be only twenty-four.

'I'm thirty-five,' he'd answered smugly, clearly pleased as punch to have shocked her.

'You pig! I hate you even more,' she'd cried, punching him playfully, then demanding the secret of his strangely youthful looks. Mitch in turn had started fondling her body and kissing her neck and ears, whilst whispering an absurdly

211

obscene explanation. After thirty seconds, she'd lost interest in the causes and surrendered with joy to the effects.

'So, have you decided,' he persisted when she didn't answer.

Dani had made her decision hours ago, but she thought Mitch deserved a little more suffering to pay him back for his deceptions and tricks. She was going to manage the hotel *and* be his lover, but she wouldn't tell him that till tomorrow. A bit more uncertainty would probably make him try *even* harder to please her . . .

Stretching luxuriously, Dani leaned over the side of the bed and picked up the nearest of the fallen documents. It looked like an analysis of some kind, but of chemical constituents, not money.

'What's this?' she enquired, instead of answering the question he'd asked her.

Brushing his shiny black hair out of his eyes, Mitch studied the document closely, thereby conclusively proving that his glasses were something of an affectation.

'It's a chemical analysis of the Bouvier Manor Spring water,' he said with a smile. 'I own a pharmaceuticals firm, and I sent a sample along to the boffins to see if the damned stuff really is an aphrodisiac . . .'

'And is it?' asked Dani as he let the paper flutter away and reached out for her body once again.

'It's inconclusive,' he murmured, sliding down against her, his hard penis caressing her thigh as his mouth went in search of her breast. 'It could be, or it couldn't be . . . There isn't a great deal of difference between the water here and anywhere else . . .' He was nibbling at her nipple now, and Dani found it hard to lie still.

212

'I don't understand it,' she gasped. 'If it isn't the water, what is it? What turns everyone here into a sex maniac?'

'God knows,' replied Mitch, lifting his face. He was grinning his demon-boy grin again, and in his eyes there was the old familiar challenge. 'Do you think we dare try a little more research?'

With that he lowered his face to her breasts once more, and started kissing them with a tenderness that awed her.

I dare, oh yes how I dare! thought Dani, pushing her fingers through his thick, silky hair, then arching her body off the bed towards his lips....

[ ]	Back in Charge	Mariah Greene	£4.99
[ ]	The Discipline of Pearls	Susan Swann	£4.99
[ ]	Arousing Anna	Nina Sheridan	£4.99

X Libris offers an eXciting range of quality titles which can be ordered from the following address:

Little, Brown and Company (UK),
P.O. Box 11,
Falmouth,
Cornwall TR10 9EN

Alternatively you may fax your order to the above address.
FAX No. 0326 376423.

Payments can be made as follows: cheque, postal order (payable to Little, Brown and Company) or by credit cards, Visa/Access. Do not send cash or currency. UK customers and B.F.P.O. please allow £1.00 for postage and packing for the first book, plus 50p for the second book, plus 30p for each additional book up to a maximum charge of £3.00 (7 books plus).

Overseas customers including Ireland please allow £2.00 for the first book plus £1.00 for the second book, plus 50p for each additional book.

NAME (Block Letters) _____

_____

ADDRESS _____

_____

_____

☐ I enclose my remittance for _____

☐ I wish to pay by Access/Visa card

Number _____

Card Expiry Date _____